William Clark

Marciano; or, The Discovery

A Tragi-comedy

William Clark

Marciano; or, The Discovery
A Tragi-comedy

ISBN/EAN: 9783744768085

Printed in Europe, USA, Canada, Australia, Japan

Cover: Foto ©Andreas Hilbeck / pixelio.de

More available books at **www.hansebooks.com**

MARCIANO;

OR,

THE DISCOVERY.

𝔄 𝔗𝔯𝔞𝔤𝔦=𝔠𝔬𝔪𝔢𝔡𝔶,

BY

WILLIAM CLARK,

ADVOCATE.

EDINBURGH:

REPRINTED FOR PRIVATE CIRCULATION.

MDCCCLXXI.

INTRODUCTORY NOTICE.

ALTHOUGH in the earlier times, dating back to the reign of King James I., moralities and religious mysteries were occasionally performed under sanction of the Church, stage plays have never been regarded with favour in Scotland, the clergy more especially being opposed to amusements generally, and imbuing their followers with the same narrow prejudice. The nearest approach to the regular drama was Sir David Lindsay's " Plesant Satyre of the Thre Estaites," which was first represented " at Lithguoe before the Kinge and Queene, and the hoole counsaile, spiritual and temporale, in the feast of the Epiphane of our Lorde, January 1539." It was subsequently acted " at Cupar, in the Playfield, on the Castle hill," and " in the Grenesyd, besyd Edinburgh, in presence of the Quene Regent." Whether from the grossly indelicate allusions throughout this piece, which were intended merely as a reflex of the popular spirit of the period, or from some other cause, arising out of the author having previously rendered himself obnoxious to Roman Catholics by promulgating the reformed belief, a council of the clergy held in the Blackfriars of Edinburgh in March 1558-59, "made an act that Sir David Lindsay's book should be abolished and burned."

James VI. interposed his authority to stay the opposition of churchmen to theatrical representations, and in 1592, 1599, and 1601 granted licences to certain English companies to perform in Scotland, but, when he succeeded to the English throne and went with his court to London, the drama was not allowed to obtain a hearing. The results of the civil wars in the reign of Charles I. kept the drama still longer a sealed book. The first gleam of the revival of a dramatic taste in Scotland did not break forth until after the Restoration, but it was only occasionally that this taste could find indulgence.

The clergy of Perth appear to have been more liberal-minded than their brethren in respect to dramatic representations, for not only during the last century was it a common thing for the scholars attending the Grammar School there, to perform plays on certain festive occasions, but in an extract from an old record of the Church of Perth, preserved in the Statistical Account of Scotland, dated June 3d 1589, "the ministers and elders give licence to plai the plai, with conditions that no swearing, banning, nor onie scurrility sal be spoken, which would be a scandal to our religion, which we profess, and for an evil example unto others. Alswa that nathing sall be added to what is in the register of the plai itself. If any one who plais sal do in the contrairie, he sal be *wardit*, and mak his public repentance." See also the Chronicle of Perth (Maitland Club) Edin. 1831, 4to.

Marciano, which after the lapse of upwards of two hundred years, is now reprinted for the first time, appears to have been the first play presented after the Restoration. This was in 1663.

The Commissioner before whom Marciano was acted was the Earl, afterwards Duke of Rothes. He received his appointment in May 1663. Besides being chosen Commissioner to the Parliament he became "Great Thesaurer of Scotland," and "came down fra court with sindry of the nobilitie that haid bene in England a long tyme befoir, upone the 15th day of Junij, being Monday, to Halyrud hous, richlie prepared for him ; at his downcuming many thowsands attending." Parliament met on the 18th June. (See Nicoll's Diary, Bannatyne Club Publications, Edin. 1836.)

The next dramatic representation took place in 1668, when Sydserf's comedy of "Tarugo's Wiles, or the Coffee-House," was brought out at the Duke of York's (James II.) theatre, said to have been the hall of the Tennis court (which was burnt down in 1774) in the Abbey, without the Watergate.

Thomas Sydserf, it would seem, continued for sometime thereafter to retain a dramatic company to represent plays and for hire, but whether he was allowed the use of the hall of the Tennis court is uncertain. From particulars educed in an action which he brought against a person named Mungo Murray in June 1689 for intruding, with personal violence, upon him and his company during rehearsal, the place of entertainment he occupied is characterized as "his hous in the Canongate, quher he keeps his theater for acteing his playes." In relation to this theatre the following of several excerpts from the note-book of Sir John Foulis, Bart. of Ravelstoun, go to prove not only the continuance of dramatic representations in Edinburgh well patronized, but that plays, despite all opposition, were elsewhere in Scotland in the custom of being performed :—

"1671, Dec. 1. A dinner at Leith to Sir James, Lady Grissell, Cristian, Antie, &c., and for the play, £11, 4s. [Scots].

" 1672, *Jan.* 26. When we went over to Bruntiland, for coatches, fraught, dinner, and the play, £20, 5s.

" 1672, *Feb.* 27. Spent at Newhaven, and Leith, and at the play, with young and old Ratho, Sir James Hay, Marg. spouse, Lady Ratho, my wife, &c., £6.

" 1672, *March* 9. Payed for myselfe, my wife, and Cristian, to see Macbeth acted, and for sweetmeats to Lady Colingtoune, Lady Margaret M'Kenzie, and others, £6, 2s."

On this occasion Macbeth must have been acted in Edinburgh for the first time, although there is no printed record of the performance of that play until 1714.

" 1672, *Jan.* 29. Drink-money to my Lord's man, and for to see the play when we came from Musselebrught with the Chancellour.

" 1672, *June* 21. To see the comedie when the Commissioner [John, Duke of Lauderdale] was ther, and for oranges for gentlewomen, £2, 8s.

" 1672, *June* 25. To let the Lady Pittaro and Sir James Sinclar's Lady see the comedie, and for oranges and cherries to them, £5, 12s. 9d.

" 1672, *Nov.* 28. To my wife and Christian to see the comedie acted, £2, 18.

" 1672, *Dec.* 21. To see Sir Solomon acted, £1, 9s."

In 1679, 1680, and 1681, when the Duke and Duchess of York, and the Princess Ann resided at Holyrood House, a company of comedians formed a part of the royal suite for private entertainment only.

Lord Fountainhall in his "Historical Observes" notes this:—" 15th Novembris 1681, being the Quean of Brittain's birth-day, it was keeped by our court at Halirud house with great solemnitie, such as bonfyres, shooting of canons, and the acting a comedy [*sic*] called *Mithridates, King of Pontus*, before ther Royall Hynesses, &c., wheirin

Ladie Anne, the Duke's daughter, and the ladies of honour ware the onlie actors."

Notwithstanding these performances were of a private nature, "not only the canonists both Protestant and Popish," his Lordship remarks, "but the very heathen roman lawyers, declared all scenicks and stage-players infamous, and will scarce admit them to the sacrament of the Lord's Supper."

Thereafter, the Revolution and the Union so disturbed men's minds that the drama was again unheard of till the year 1714.

For subsequent notices of the Scotish drama during the eighteenth century, see Fragmenta Scoto Dramatica, Edin. 1835, 12mo, and Jackson's Scotish Stage.

Marciano appears to have been acted only once, although doubtless from the circumstance alone of amateurs sustaining the several characters it could not fail to be received with favour. The Biographia Dramatica states that the author was one of the performers, but which character he performed has not been suggested.

Amateur acting, although pretty common throughout English towns and villages, especially at Christmas-tide, from an early period, received its initiative in Scotland on the occasion of the production of Marciano; but, while amateurs have been greatly supported in the southern parts of our island, it has not received much encouragement in the north. The prejudice against theatrical representations in Scotland has not quite died away even in the present (so-called) enlightened times.

The author of Marciano is believed to have been Mr William Clark or Clerke, a member of the Scotish bar. He was one of those advocates who, along with John Lauder, afterwards Lord Fountainhall, and others, was

"debarred" from practising in the Court by reason of their
having asserted the right of appeal against "the Lords of
Session their sentences of injustice." Proclamation of
banishment from Edinburgh against those debarred advocates was made by the king's authority 6th Oct. 1674.
This sentence was reversed in January 1676. On the 10th
of that month, Fountainhall in noticing their restoration to
office, adds, "our Collection and Observes return to their
former orderly channell." See Fountainhall's Historical
Notices, 1835, 4to. Also the Court of Session Garland,
Edin. 1871, 8vo. Lord Fountainhall has also recorded the
following incidents, which, if true, do not exhibit his "co-
mate in exile," Mr Clark, in the most honourable light :—

"In Dec. 1674, William Cockburne, merchant, was in
the Secret Councell sentenc't to the cock stule, and banish't
the Louthians, and declared infamous, for having defamed
my Ladie Oxenfuird in hir honor both in a letter, which
Mr William Clerk, advocat, his brother-in-law, treacher-
ously gave up to my Lord Oxenfuird, and in discourse."

Five years after this, Cockburn "gave in a bill to the
Secret Councell representing that his Majesty, by his late
indemnity, had pardoned all pasquills, infamous libells, and
sentences of the like nature, and remitted them both *quoad
vindictam publicam et privatam*, and commanded his indemnity
to be extended by his judges, with all favour and latitude,
&c. ; and theirfor craved their Lordships would declare he
was free theirby, and discharge Oxenfuird to trouble him,
&c." His bill was refused. "The king's pardon in
England does not comprehend private offences." Fountainhall, vol. i., p. 236. Still Cockburn appears to have
"broken his confinement," and being fined at Privy Council
5000 merks was imprisoned until he could pay it.

"18th May, 1682. At Privy Counsell, (the Duke of

York being parted for London on the 5th of May before) upon a complaint given in by Ruthven of Gairne against Mr Wm. Clerk, advocat, bearing that he had hitherto keeped up all his estate and papers, and therfor craving he might be desired to give up the papers, and restore him his rents. Tho' this was civill, yet because of the long vacance, he being ane advocat, who would decline inferior courts, the Lords referred the count and reckoning to the Session; but in the meantime modified 50 lb. sterling to be payed yearly by Mr William to him during the dependance (if Mr William should prolong it) beginning the 1 terme's payment at Whitsunday coming. Mr William reclamed much, offering instantly to count with him."

"20th January 1687. Ruthven of Gairn's complaint against Mr William Clark, advocat, is heard, and Mr Clark fred from paying him the 50 lb. sterling formerly decerned, till he first find sufficient caution *judicio sisti et judicatum solvi;* if, in the count and reckoning betwixt them, Mr Clark be not found his debtor, then to refund it." What was the issue of this suit has not been ascertained.

The families of Clerke or Clark probably emanated from Banff, where, from an early date they held a position of consequence. The following document introduces one of the name:—

"Instrumentum possessionis quinque Mercarum vitalis redditus in Banff factum Domino Gulielmo Clerke pro docendo Scholam Gramaticalem ibidem sua durante vita. Dated 6 March 1526."

This William Clerke was a man of substance, having a house and garden his own property, in the Burgh, or as it is sometimes called, "Urbs" of Banff,—at that date undoubtedly a place of great importance, and containing many inhabitants. It is not unworthy of remark that prior to this date, and long after it, there was hardly a tenement in the place that had not a garden attached to it—a fact showing that the belief in the want of knowledge of horticulture in that part of Scotland is not warranted. Charters and documents exist to shew also that families of the highest rank and antiquity had their residence in that Royal Burgh.

In two Banff charters, 1542-43, the name of Sir William Clerk is spelt with an "e" in one of them, while in the other it is spelt with an "a." The same individual who was master of the Grammar School is in another charter described as proprietor of certain gardens " adjacent to the Guis haugh."

In Douglas's Baronage a genealogy is given of the family of the Clerks of Pennicuik, who are said to have been, somewhere about the year 1640 or before, traders in Montrose or Dundee. They acquired wealth during the Civil War, as well as the estate of Pennicuik from the ancient family of that ilk—the chief of which subsequently became proprietor of the estate of Roman in the county of Peebles. The Clerks, however, seem to have adopted a portion of their armorial bearings, and the motto " Free for a blast," being the tenure by which it is understood they hold the lands from the Crown.

The Clerks of Pennicuik, like many other families, during the reign of Charles the II., who were connected with the City of Edinburgh, obtained considerable political influence, and in 1679 were created Baronets by his patent in the person of John. This gentleman had a son (the third) called William—the supposed Author of Marciano—who married the heiress of Maxwell of Middleby, the direct descendant of whom, Mr Clerk Maxwell (now deceased), was a Member of the Faculty of Advocates at Edinburgh in the year 1817.

Another Clerk of the same family is mentioned in Wodrow's Analecta, and in the Analecta Scotica will be found a most singular ghost story, extracted from that source, which may, upon examination, create some interest.

William Clark died before 16th November 1699, as the minutes of the Faculty of Advocates that day record the presentation "to that body by Mr Roderick Mackenzie" of certain of the manuscripts of the deceased William Clerke. Those manuscripts cannot now be found.

The rarity of the book, apart from its merits, which are by no means of a common order, having rendered Marciano of value to the Antiquary, a limited reprint was considered desirable.

A copy of Marciano was sold at the sale of the library of Mr James William Dodd of the Theatre Royal, Drury Lane, "consisting of a fine collection of old plays, old poetry, romances, history, Belles lettres, miscellanies, comic and humorous books, &c., &c." which passed under the hammer of Messrs Leigh and Sotheby in January 1797, occupying nine days. It was classed under "anonymous authors," No. 966 in the catalogue, and fetched £1, a sum which, considered relatively with the prices obtained for the earlier editions of Shakespeare's Plays, would at the present day represent more than ten times that amount.

There was a copy, perhaps the same copy, No. 822 in David Constable's catalogue, the contents of which were sold in January 1827 by Sotheby. It was purchased by Thorpe for £4, 14s. 6d. It was described " green morocco, g. l., rare." but was in very poor condition otherwise.

There is a copy in the Bodleian Library.

That from which the present reprint has been effected appears to have been acquired for the Library of the Faculty of Advocates by Mr Thomas Ruddiman, the learned antiquary, while librarian to that body. It had previously belonged to Mr Robert Mylne, a writer in Edinburgh, whose extensive collection of books and manuscripts was of a most curious and valuable description, although not quite so highly prized during his time as it would be now; and it is chiefly owing to his industry that Scotish Literary Antiquities of importance have been preserved until the present day. Mr Mylne, during a long life, transcribed numerous manuscripts for his own use, and these, as well as his books and broadsides, he was in the habit of annotating. He died on the 21st Dec. 1747, at the age of 103, although the Scots Magazine of the period makes him two years older. "He enjoyed his sight and the exercise of his understanding till a little before his death, and was buried on his birth-day." He is said to have been related to Sir Robert Milne of Barnton, then an influential gentleman, and concerned with the revenues of the City of Edinburgh. His political leaning was towards the Jacobites, and he is accused by Sir Walter Scott, in the introduction to Lord Fountainhall's "Chronological Notes of Scotish Affairs," of having interpolated and corrupted the original manuscript "to express his partial feelings in that character." Sir Walter adds:—"The Diary appears to have fallen into Milne's hands after Lord Fountainhall's death in 1724; and it is but fair to him to state that he appears to have had no purpose of passing his alterations for a part of the text, but only that of connecting and adding to it in his own name. His remarks are sometimes both shrewd and sarcastic; and though they may be considered as impairing the historical authenticity of the work, they rather add to than diminish its interest as a picture of the times."

Of the poetic merits of the Play it may suffice to call

attention to the several lyrics throughout, but more especially to the song in the third scene of the third act,

"So, so,
Lo lillies fade, before the roses show
Themselves in bow-dye," &c.

The character "Manduco, an arrogant Pedant" is well drawn. It may probably have been suggested by Pedantius, the principal of the Latin comedy so called, which was entered in the books of Stationers' Hall in 1630, and then performed at Trinity College, Cambridge. It had been frequently acted previously, even antecedent to 1591. M. Wingfield is said to have been the author. It was printed at London in 1631, 18mo, with two engravings, one of "Dromodotus" Philosophus, the other of "Pendantius" Pædagogus. They are in appropriate costumes of the period. The former is in the attitude of demonstrating some proposition on his fingers, at the same time exclaiming, "Videtur quod sic;" while Pedantius on the opposite print, facing him, with a birch dangling in his right hand, gives vent to "as in presenti." Behind him are two of his scholars in college costume.

Allusion is made, figuratively, by Marciano, to children's hobby-horses, which would appear, at the date of the play, not to have been entirely made of wood, but stuffed like dolls—a hint worthy the attention of modern toy-makers.

In Arabella's soliloquy in the seventh scene of the fourth act she appeals to the gods to hear her "ardent votes," which, although possibly a misprint for "ardent vows," the editor did not feel himself justified in altering.

The poetic muse of Mr Clark led him, some twenty years after the appearance of Marciano, into "fresh fields and pastures new," for in 1685 there issued from the press of the heir of Andrew Anderson at Edinburgh, a small folio volume titled " The Grand Tryal, or Poetical Exercitations upon the book of Job; wherein, suitable to each text of that sacred book, a modest explanation and continuation of the several discourses contained in it is attempted by William Clark."

In adopting such a subject it may be he had found that, even during the days of the merry Monarch, dramatic literature could not obtain a footing in Scotland so as to render it an acceptable or remunerative pursuit, and that deeming it more expedient and to his better interest to "assume a virtue though he had it not" had attempted to glorify himself in the eyes of the strict adherents of the Church, who regarded stage-plays as a device of the evil one, by turning his attention to more ghostly subjects, and seizing upon a theme more consonant with the prevailing current of their thoughts. In poetry and romance he is the most successful author who does not attempt to convey instruction, but who can place in a judicious light such pictures and imagery as his readers are already familiar with.

Alexander Campbell thus remarks in his Introduction to the History of Poetry in Scotland, Edin. 1798, 4to:—

" During the latter part of the seventeenth century scarcely anything was relished in Scotland unless it was larded plentifully with the ' marrow of divinity;' hence the meagreness of profane productions, in the long lent of innocent hilarity. The muses were suffered to roam at large, unless any one of them thrumbed the harp of King David for the spiritual comfort of pious covenanters."

This " Grand Tryal" consists of 370 pages, and is dedicated to James, Earl of Perth, Lord Drummond and Stobhall, Lord High Chancellor of the Kingdom of Scotland— that nobleman being, the author remarks, " supream Judge of that illustrious Court upon which my profession as a

Lawyer has afforded me a dependence now these many years." He further gives it as a reason for rushing into print, " especially being encouraged to it by your lordship's generous perusal and approbation of some of the sheets in private."

Mr Clark does not seem to have succeeded so well in his sacred as in his secular poetry. As a specimen, his description of the end of a "Man of Sin" redolent of original but fantastic imagery, may be quoted :—

" Now after he is fall'n, pray let us see
What will the state of this poor creature be ?
It shall be low, it shall be poor indeed,
His children shall from beggars beg their bread,
And from their father's slaves compassion plead.
   Then for his person (pity him who will)
He soon becomes *a horrid spectacle,*
His flesh is *larded* with his youthful sins,
And in his vigrous years old age begins
To seize upon him.

  .   .   .   .

So this poor wretch now *paralytick* grown
With *tottering head,* and *joynts* all overflown
With *Goutish humours, teeth all hanging loose*
Within their sockets : a distilling *nose,*
Eyes full of brackish liquor : *shoulders* stooping,
Under-lip in a constant spittle drooping :
Lungs with a sharp, and wasting cough opprest,
Which doth bereave him of his nightly rest,
Pump'd up the wind-pipes, with *a raging froath,*
In lobs and parcels issuing from his mouth.
His skin with boils, and ulcers diaper'd,
(Of his lascivious sports the sad reward)
His *Stomach* useless, and his *Bowels* weary
With th' torture of a constant *disentery.*
His *legs* now rotting to the bones apace
In a consuming *Eresypelas.*
Som' *dozen issues* in his shoulders, arms,
And neck appearing, *like so many charms*

And spells upon his body: all his *veins*
Choak'd with a *slymy pituite,* his *reins*
Buried in sand, which squandring everywhere,
Along the channels of each *ureter,*
Mix'd with some *rugged peebles,* doth so stop
Those conduits in their course.

. . . . .

With *hands* by drunken excess in his youth,
So *trembling,* that they scarce can to his mouth
Convey his food : *such swellings in his feet,*
As, when in cut-out shooes he walks in street,
Amongst the *busie crowd* he dares not go,
Lest some perhaps might tread upon *his toe.*
But with great leasure by shop-doors doth crawl,
Contemn'd, abhorr'd, and pointed at by all.

. . . . .

Here, here's the end of him, who takes delite
In acts of sin, *whose curious appetite*
Feeds upon sin, dress'd up with sauce of youth,
Which makes it taste like honey in the mouth.''

The impression of " Marciano " has been limited to seventy-five copies.

W. H. LOGAN.

BERWICK-ON-TWEED, 31*st March* 1871.

MARCIANO;

OR,

THE DISCOVERY.

A

TRAGI-COMEDY,

Acted with great applause , before His *Majesties* high Commissioner, and others of the Nobility, at the Abby of *Holyrud-house*, on St. *Johns* night :

By a company of Gentlemen.

Segnius irritant animum demissa per aurem,
Quam quæ sunt oculis subjecta fidelibus——
Hor. *de art. Poet.*

Edinburgh , Printed in the year , 1663.

To all humours.

IT was eafie to caft the horofcope of this Peece before it peep'd into the world, it being to appear in a Country, where the cold air of mens affeftions nips fuch buds in their very infancy: But, it was refolv'd it fhould live, maugre all the foul-mouth'd, detrafting cenfures of fome modern Criticks, who, labouring to deprive this of all applaufe, do render all others of this kind defpicable in the fight of, otherwayes more ingenuous perfons then themfelves, fuch as prefume upon a monopoly of wit granted to them and their company, who, like to the Spaniard, fcorns all perfumes, but what his own Country produces, do extort a larger Preface then was really intended. Although then, it is not ordinar to apologize for Playes in general, at the publifhing of any particular one ; Yet, becaufe this now appears as a City-fwaggarer in a Country-church, where feldom fuch have been extant ; and that the peevifh prejudice of fome perfons, who know nothing beyond the principles of bafe, greazy, arrogant, illiterate Pedants, who, like the grafs-hoppers of *Egypt*, fwarm in every corner of this Nation, and plague all the youth accordingly, is fuch, that they cannot have patience to hear of a Comedy, becaufe they never fee one afted : For thefe reafons, you may confider Playes in their antiquity, ufe and dignity, and then, *ingenuè mecum agat Zoilus*. We read of fuch praftices among the Grecians fince the firft Olympiad, now more then

A 2   two

two thousand years ago; from whom they were transferred to the Romans, by them had in such high veneration, that the greatest Emperors and Princes amongst them, as *Julius Cæsar* and others, upon the festival dayes, have made experiment of their gallantry by acting: and it is esteemed yet so little derogatory from the quality of a Prince, (far lesse of a Gentleman) to appear at solemnities upon the Stage, that it is laudably practised amongst our Christian Monarchs to this day.

The use which may be reaped of playes is so evident, that unless a man mistrust his very senses, he cannot but confesse, that to see, in a well acted Tragedy, the fatal ends of such as commit notorious murders, rapins, and other licentious vices represented, would terrifie any man whatsoever from attempting the like. In a Comedy, where ordinarly the paltry vices of the age, such as the Court-vanity and prodigality, the City covetousnefs, or the Country-simplicity, &c. are extraordinarly taxed, many are deterred from what formerly they hugg'd, seeing their darling crimes exposed upon a publick Stage to the mockerie of the world: and hence, he who is even but the least converfant with the hatefull humours of both Sexes of our times, after perusal, may guesse why this carries the Title of *The Discovery*. Besides, Playes incite the youth to imitate the vertuous actions of their Predeceffors, as *Alexander* was stirr'd up by representation of *Achilles* actions, *Achilles* by those of *Thefeus*, &c. with feveral other examples, whereof pregnant History can give an ample account. Nor is the perfection in acting less beneficial to the Commonwealth: For, we read how all the young Nobility of *Greece* were train'd up in this noble exercise, that they might be the better enabled to demean themselves handfomly in forraign Embassies, or such like imployments: and we fee even in our dayes

dayes, how all fuch as are educat in the Jesuit Schools, where no lefs then amongft publick Actors the Stage is dayly trod, gain an unfpotted reputation of compleat Orators throughout all the Chriftian world. And the defficiency (or rather wilfull contempt of this education) is the reafon why many of our pretenders to wit, now a dayes forfooth, either whiftle of a tedious harrangue with no more motion then a ftatue, or elfe ufe fuch a canting conftrained tone, with fuch ridiculous grimaffees, as they feem rather to imitate a Mountebanks Zany, in his apifh geftures, then to afpire to the title of accomplifhed Orators. Wheras to deliver a fpeech naturally, that the action may fute the words, and the words the action ; although diffonant to· the pedantry of this age, who vote down the ufe of Stage-playes (as they call them) for no other reafon, but becaufe in them, fuch pilfring ftinkards as themfelves, are often difcovered in their own colours ; fo ridiculous in their imperious behaviour, that none fave them felves (whofe innate ftupidity doth much excufe their impudence) cannot but fee it and abhor it ; although difsonant, I fay, to their humours, yet is, by the approbation of all the intelligent world, the chiefeft ingredient of an ingenuous Orator.

The dignity of Playes is fuch, as it hath been the ftudy of the greatest Monarchs who ever flourifhed, to encourage the wit of their respective ages in fuch active performances, not only by their open countenance, but likewife private favours beftowed on the managers of fuch exercifes, as many fair monumental Theaters built by the moft eminent perfons of the world, in their very ruins, do yet eloquently teftifie.

Nor doth there any thing appear in holy Writings to impugn thefe affertions. For (which is remarkable) Playes of all forts, did never fo much flourifh throughout all the

Territories

Territories of the Roman Empire, as in the dayes of our bleffed Saviour and his Apostles; yet we never read that He,
or any of them (otherwayes impartial reprovers of their con-
temporary enormities, did ever, either directly, or indirectly
tax this innocent and ufefull recreation : But on the contra-
ry, inveighed againft fuch hypocrits, as deluded the world
with a vain fhow of piety, fuch as are now our fneaking
detractors of the Stage, who, its probable) only hate Playes,
becaufe fuch pleafant fpectacles divert the current of our,
otherwayes melancholly imaginations, and hinder people from
dreaming on rebellion, which our late proceedings may at
large inftruct : For no fooner had thofe hell-hounds, affafsi-
nats of our liberties, fnatch'd the very reins of Government
into their hands, but as foon they thought it expedient to
vote down all Scenick Playes, fo that they fhould fuffer in
that fame fentence with Monarchy ; upon whom they have
fuch a dependance, that at the thrice aufpicious reftauration
of our Royal Soveraign, they were not only by him re-efta-
blifhed, but also more glorioufly adorned with priviledges,
then formerly.

The main intent of this enfuing Tragi-comedy, was to
fmatter at a complement, for that noble *Hero*, whofe merits
claim more at the hands of all *Appollo's* fubjects, then the
ftock of their inventions will ever be able to refound ; who,
as he hath proved himfelf (fince firft he was entrufted) a
zealous propagator of the Royal Intereft, fo hath appear'd a
very noble Patron to all true wit and gallantry whatfoever.
But leaft it fhould feem too ferious for the pallats of thofe,
who expected nothing from the Stage but mirth : It was
thought fit to interlude it with a comick tranfaction. So that
being tyed to two different plots, without the fpeciall concur-
rence of a certain ingenuous Gentleman, to whofe induftry
this Play owes much of its perfection, it had been a diffi-
cult

cult task to have arrived at a happy Cataftrophe, feeing how
hard it is to carry on two different plots in one fingle Play,
is not unknown to any, who know what belongs to the
Stage.

Let this then fuffice the judicious Reader, As for fuch
of a feeming ferious, but real fawcy apprehenfion, who condemn this, as an inconfiderate youthfull frolick; when indeed, fuch clogs of Parnaffus, are as fo much roft-beef to
their fqueamifh ftomacks; whofe *calidum naturale*, can
digeft nothing more heavy than bawdry Ballads, fcurrilous
Sonnets, and fuch water-works of Poetry: 'tis below *Phæbus*
to cudgel them, and any, fave pitifull, threed-bare, cring-
ing, indigent, mercenary dablers, to flatter them. Let them
live and die in the trenches of their own nefty ignorance,
whilft all lovers of mirth and wit, may dayly challenge the
refpeéts of,

Their really devoted.

Dramatis Personæ.

CLeon, *Duke of* Florence.
Marciano, *a noble Siennois, his General.*
Strenuo, Marciano's *friend.*
Borasco, *Captain of the rebels guard.*
Caffio, ⎱
Leonardo, ⎰ *two noble Gentlemen of quality.*
Pantaloni, ⎱
Becabunga, ⎰ *two rich gulls, in favour with the Ladies*
Manduco, *an arrogant Pedant, challenging power over*
Becabunga.
Two Courtiers.
Jaylor.
A Servant, Partuysans, Drums, Trumpets, Souldiers, &c.

Women.

Arabella, *A Siennois Lady, beloved of* Marciano.
Chrysolina, ⎱
Marionetta, ⎰ *two Ladies of honour.*
The Scæn, Florence.

MARCIANO;

O R,

THE DISCOVERY.

Actus primus Scæna prima.

*A noyſe within, Trumpets, Drums, Piſtols,
Shot, Swords claſh, &c.*

Enter Marciano, *wounded, chaffing,* &c.

————Oſt——By heavens——all loſt,
All our hopes blaſted
By *Jove*, without hope of recovery.
O gods, commiſerate our deſpicable eſtate.
        A noiſe within as before,
                     Exit *haſtily.*
           Enters again.

Oh heavens ! this day were we at puſh of pike
For our publike liberty——Now we are at our wits end
For our private ſafety.——
        A noyſe within cry, they fly, they fly,
Harke, what a hideous noyſe——this fatal day
Hath cancell'd all our former victories,
Never to be remembred——in this hour
Our ancient ſplendour ſuffers ſad ecclipſe.
——*They fly*——*They fly*——Oh what a dismal word !
How unaccuſtom'd——*Siennois* to fly ;
True *Siennois*——ſuch as had vowed their lives
A victime for their publike liberty,

           B   To

To fly, like duſt before mechanick ſlaves;
Such as while now never knew other armes,
Then forks or ſhovels——Do the gods intend
To revel in our miſeries!——and prove
Strange paradoxes to the credulous world!
That abjeſt, baſe, unmannag'd Varlets thus
Should overcome the Cavalry of *Siena*?
A thing unheard of! O! accurſed wretches,
Whoſe too politick pates firſt hatcht theſe warres;
You are leaſt ſharers here. My Prince and I
Muſt ſuffer this reproach ——I ſlight my wounds;
—— But O! my honour loſt.——I'le bear it ſtoutly:
—— Up then my ſpirits, be not you dejeſted;
There's ſomething yet to care for——there's no time
Now to complain : heaven knows what juſt deſignes
We undertook; though with unequal ſucceſs.
Wee've done what lay in humane power—*Piſtoia*
Bear witneſs, where ſo many inſolent rebells
Have found this day their ſepulchre : thy fields
Can teſtifie how dear ſome ſold their lives.
And thou the Enſigne of all noble ſouls ⎫
Make affidavit of this dayes behaviour. ⎬ *Holds up his ſword.*
—— Now to my generous Prince, whom cruel fates,
Have levell'd with my ſelf—Him will I ſearch,
That if my fates require my quick departure
For *Stygian* lakes : as in my life I've been
Eminent in his ſervice, I may now,
Dying couragiouſly in his preſence, have
His royal Paſs-port and Teſtificate,
To raiſe my honour, and condole my fate.

                                        Exit.

Scæna.

Scæna Secunda.

Enter Borasco *with Souldiers.*

Bor.——SO now the day's our own——but yet the Duke
Escap'd—*Marciano* not prisoner !
The victory is not such as I expected.
But come, my *Mirmydons,*——wee'l not give over ;
Let's, with a party of our choicest horse,
Make narrow search for *Marciano* :
For, if we find him not, we must not think
To gain the Generals favour.——Come, my Boyes,
He hath attempted oft to strip the Senate
Of their new power, and so destroy us all ;
Whose hopes are nourished by the present wars :
So that if you shall catch him, you may sure
Expect a great reward :——his excellency,
The brave Lord *Barbaro* will hugg you for it.

                      Exit *with Sould.*

Scæna Tertia.

Enter Marciano *solus.*

O *Florence !* don't insult at this dayes success,
   This unnatural victory over thy lawfull Prince
Will quickly make thee sensible of unnatural
And intolerable Tyranny : that *Ichneumon,*
Who now tickles thee in all thy desires
Will stop thy breath at length, whilst thy good Prince,
Whom thou can blame for nothing but misfortune,
Shall yet be more unfortunate in seeing
Thee too unfortunate.——But, I perceive
The main designe of this preposterous war,·
Love and ambition muzles humane souls ;

So that when private Subjects covet honour
And power, their lawfull Prince muſt quit his Throne,
No matter for what reaſon, ſince they mean
Some reformation ; as if private preferment
Were inconſiſtent with all Monarchy.
——But what ! 'tis unſeaſonable for me t'expoſtulate.
My noble Prince (goodneſs protect him ſtill)
Is gone for *Savoy* ; I am here commanded
To rally thoſe few forces I can find,
With ſlender hopes——but yet I'le do my beſt
To proſecute his Royal orders——ſo,
Good Subjects votes aſſiſt me——'tis reſolv'd,
   For while Dame nature does allow me breath,
   I'le ſerve my Prince—nought ſhall excuſe but death.

Exit.

Scæna Quarta.

Enter Caſſio, Leonardo, *as at* Florence.

Caſſ. ——O ! *Leonardo*——How doſt do Boy ?
        Leon. Caſſio——thou art the man I was ſeeking, welcome effaith, and how Prethee ? *Caſſ.* Well.

Leon. As well as the Ladies will permit thee ?——ha.

Caſſ. Yes indeed——but how goes all with you——what news do'ſt hear ?

Leon. Bad news effaith, all our hopes are now periſh'd, it is for certain that the Duke is beat at *Piſtoia* ; whether he hath eſcaped or not himſelf, is not yet known.

Caſſ. ——Sad ——truſt me 'tis moſt sad, but, prethee, who ſhall be Duke now do'ſt think, when they have rejected him, who by law of inheritance was their lawfull·Prince.

Leon. Why——thou,——if thou bee'ſt weary of thy life ; for a Prince now a dayes muſt raign no longer then his Subjects pleaſe his government——men now begin to act real Tragedies.

Caſſ.

Caſſ. Good; but how does thy learned cocks-comb judge of the event of all our preſent broyls?

Leon. Why, juſt as a ſober Drawer does of a company of young gulls inflaming the reckoning beyond the faculties of their pockets :———they will look pittifully, when the bill is produc'd———for they muſt pay for all.

Caſſ. How! do'ſt think our ſtate-mountebanks will not agree?

Leon. Yes, for a while they may, like heiffers in the yoke, but when once got looſe, they'll puſh at one another.

Caſſ. Well———no more of that ſtring; theſe diſtracted times, I fear, will afford ſuch diſcourſes every day———how does thy Miſtreſs, the Lady you know of,———ha?

Leon. ———Why, faith as unreaſonable as ever.

Caſſ. How! unreaſonable———

Leon. Yes———unreaſonable, ſhe will admit of no tearms whatſoever, ſo that I fear I ſhall be forc'd to ſtorm her : 'ſlid, I can have ſcarce liberty to ſurvey her very parapet and out-works for fear of a thing (I do not know what they mean now a dayes) ſuſpicion, I think ſhe calls it ; and for thee, I beleeve thou art in no better condition, for her Siſter, thy Miſtreſs (otherwayes in my opinion plyable) is rul'd by her, and both by an old urinal-peeping, onyon-breath'd hag, whom they call the Counteſſe of *Saromanca* forſooth, ſo that now ſhe is impregnable.

Caſſ. A devil ſhe is, 'ſlid, I think it is become an epidemical diſeaſe amongſt that ſexe, they intend, I think, to imitate the times, and erect a new Commonwealth of themſelves, excluding all maſculine ſociety, and ſo be call'd *the new aſſembly of zeal-copyholders.*

Leon. Yes, yes, for now they hold it a cryme to court.

Caſſ. Since Monarchy fell, that trade is totally decayed, thou muſt now either Marry at firſt ſight or elſe march off; as if who ſhould throw the Dye for a maydenhead, Boy.

Leon. Goodneſs, I think, by and by, we ſhall be conſtrained to make love to one another. and ſo thou ſhalt be my Miſtreſs, *Caſſio*; for our modern Criticks will not allow us womens fleſh, even upon holy-dayes.

Caſſ. True———for all the Ladies in *Florence* have a ſpice of this diſeaſe is there no remedy for't, do'ſt think?

Leon.

Leon. None but patience, ſtay while Fortune turn up her wheel again, and then the Ladyes may turn up.

Caſſ. What ! their Petticoats ?

Leon. No——I have not ſayd that yet, I mean may ſmile upon us more than they do : for now wee muſt not so much as ſee any Lady.

Caſſ. No——why I hope they will yet admit of a viſit in civility ?

Leon. No——by no means, *Caſſio*, thou muſt not name ſuch a he-reſie as a viſit, for thou may'ſt hinder other ſuitors : Remember that, Boy.

Caſſ. You ſay right——But who comes here ?}
Leon. I think they are women.
Caſſ. Or elſe two things ſhufled in the forme
of women : doſt know 'em *Leonardo* ?
Leon. Know 'em, why, who can know them
thus, ſuch maſquerades under their vailes are like}
nnns at the grate, they may ſee us, but wee cannot ſee them.

Enter Chryſolina, aud Marionetta uſher'd by Panta-loni, *at ſight of* Caſſ. and Leon. *they pull down their vailes, traverſe, &c.*

Exeunt

Caſſ. True, for there is no way elſe to diſcover them, but by ſmelling ; and what ſmell women have now a dayes, faith, I cannot tell.

Leon. Smell, ſayſt thou ; they have a moſt acute ſmell, a wo-man can now a dayes ſmell a mans love to her, before ever poſſibly he be in love with any ; I was rejeſted by a lady laſt day, before ever I knew her well ; yet ſuch was the imagination that ſhe had of my reſpeſts, that ſhe entertained her companions with the relation of my adventures for her——you will think that ſtrange.

Caſſ.—Strange ! —No faith, I hope, by progreſſe of time, they will conceive by the meer wind of report, and ſo wee ſhall have a hopefull race of young *Florentine*-jennets, as light-heel'd as thoſe of *Spain*, I warrand yow : but, prethee, what was that Lady, you talk'd of ?

Leon. Why, the little handſome *Donazella*, what do you call her, on the other ſyde of the river ?

Caſſ. Ho——Ho——I know her, a noble Lady eſſaith, but I am ſorry, that ſhe is infeſted with that diſeaſe, ſhe ſeemes to have a ſpark of wit.

Leon.

The Difcovery. 7

Leon. Tufh, 'tis become a plague, *Caffio*, a very plague; do'ft not know the gentelman, who was rejected of a Lady, having no other evidence of his affection then the carrying of a letter from one of her friends to her, wherein he was recommended to her acquaintance, which as a trophee of her conquefts fhe did impart to her *hearts-conquerour*—and yet a Lady of admirable qualities.——Men now a dayes breed their female children, as the *Chinefes* do their wives, or the *Grand-fignior* his concubines, clofe at home.

Caff. But, prethee, did'ft know that fame peece of foppery, who attended them who by his garbe would feeme to challenge the title of a man?

Leon. Know him, why, who does not know him; 'tis *Signior Pantaloni*, the rich city-gull, whofe golden fleece dazles the eyes of all the Ladyes in Toun, to whofe chamber he is almoft as welcome as a young batchelour of Divinity, who hath lately paft his tryalls, is to a zealous widow of ten months ftanding, that would faine repeat her former allegiance, and tafte the game again—— But come, you fhall go along with me to the Lady *Chryfolina*, there I hope wee fhall have fome favour, if wee get acceffe, I mean.

Caff. ——I, with all my heart, but that's the queftion.

Exeunt.

Scæna Quinta.

Enter Pantaloni, *with* Chryfolina *and* Marionetta.

Pant. I take it fo indeed, Ladies, you muft excufe me if I do you the honour to vifit you fometimes; for my mother fayes, Son, faith fhe, it is high time you were married——I hope you know my meaning.

Chryf. Sir, you fhall be welcome.

Pant. I hope fo indeed :——For, I vow I would never defire a handfomer wife than you are.——I proteft, Miftrefs, you are very handfome, though I fay it that fhould not fay it.

Mar. You flatter highly, Sir.

Pant. Not indeed.

Chryf.

Chryf. Well, Sir, as for your vifit, I fhall admit it; but for marriage——you know——

Pant. Ho——I know well enough, you are governed by your friends; but I fhall tickle them I warrand you, let me alone for that.

Mar. It is the fafeft way, Sir.

Pant. So——then forfooth, fince I know the way to your Chamber, I will come and fee you every day; now becaufe my mother is fick and taking phyfick, I muft go home and keep company with her, elfe I'l affure you, I would not leave you thus——farewell.

Exit.

Mar. You fee them Gentelmen, *Caffio* and *Leonardo*, as we paffed along, Sifter?

Chryf. But I hope they did not know us, Sifter, 'tis not fit we entertain them, they are not matches for us.

Mar. But I warrand you, they'l render us a vifit fhortly.

Chryf. I fhould rather wifh they would abftain, Sifter, you know our friends will not relifh it well; I fhould be very well content of this *Signior Pantaloni* for my husband; I hope no body hears us.

Mar. True, for although the others may be Gentelmen of good parts, yet I know wee are defign'd for them *Signiors;* fo the Lady *Saromanca* told me laft day.

Chryf. And wee muft follow their advice you know Sifter.

Mar. Yes indeed, and reafon for it.

Enter Manduco haftily.

Man. Hum——*etiam confabulantes inveni:* I have it in my pocket, that will afford them new cogitations.

Chryf. Mr. *Manduco*, you are welcome, pray, how does my aunt?

Man. I have a little negotiation with you in private; for I am legate from *Signior Becabunga*, (my fometimes pupill) as more amply fhall briefly appear. And how think *}* *takes out a Let-* you——marry thus, here's a letter for you—— *}* *ter out of a to-*

Chryf. I hope he is in good health, Sir. *}* *bacco-box.*

Man. O! yes, he is valetudinary, herein he prefents (as I conjecture

jecture) his amorous fervitude to you both; he will be in Town next week, for I'l affure you he flagitates to fee you: I hope you will afford him gracious entertainment——hum——hum——

Chryf. He fhall be welcome, Sir.

Man. I will affure you, Ladies, he is an adolefcent of eximious candour and egregious integrity: I have been at much pains and labour in educating him, I may fay, ever fince his pubertie: but now that he is come to the years of intelligency, I have given him over——

Mar. He will make us in love with him e're we fee him.

Man. But, for your further fatisfaction, I shall, *pauciffimis*, infinuate to you the method of his education.——*Primo*, then, when he came under my gubernation, which was about the year of his age, *Anno Domini*, (let me fee) *milleffimo, fexcentefimo, quadragefimo fexto*, it being then Leap-year; he was, *inquam*, a very perverfe youth, vitiat in his behaviour, knowing nothing but what he had learned amongft the *ancilla's* (what d'you call 'em) Chambermaids.

Chryf. Now, Sifter, you fhall have him anatomized to you.

Man. But, fo foon as I took him in hand, I did fo belabour his *nates* with my *ferula*, that *profecto* I have whipped him, whip'd him thus——for half an hour together, until his abundant lachrymation had mov'd compaffion: but, I knew that was the only way to difciplinate him——

Chryf. Indeed, Sir——

Man.——So, I fay, having taught him his *Orthographia, Etymologia* and *Profodia*, having always a follicitous eye over his behaviour: I did learn him to make his reverence, not as your *Monfieurs* do, but more gravely in this manner; next, how to }*congees*, &c. take a Lady by the hand;——So——afterwards how to kifs,—— in this fafhion——

Mar. A pretty method indeed.

Man. I gave him, as I fay, wholfom admonitions, cautions, inftructions, and now and then fome little exhortations. *Primo*, Not to be garrulous; for, (believe me, Ladies) *Vir fapit, qui pauca loquitur*; you are always wifeft when you hold your peace. And then with that gefture to difcourfe, gravely, as you fee me,

C   and

and like a School-man ; (for, I have been fometimes *Hypodidafca-lus* in the great School of *Florence, imo Hypodidafculus,* Ladies,) but, as I faid, I learned him to be concinne and terfe in his habit, with hair in the fame longitude, as you fee mine. *Secundo,* How to keep a clean mundified nofe, not with his fleeve, but with his *fudarium,* or handkercher————

Mar. He intends to weary us I think.

Man. Tertio, As I faid————(*hoc agatur ferio*) *tertio,* as I faid, *tertio, inquam,* to eat his meat with a great deal of circumfpeétion and neatly; that is to fay, with one finger and his thumb ————thus————*Quarto,* To contain himfelf *à capite fcalpendo* ; from fcratching of his head, (give ear I befeech you, Ladies, for it concernes you.)

Mar. He thinks we are his Schollars.

Chryf. Peace, Sifter, let us hear him out.

Man. Quarto, As I faid, (take heed) *Quinto,* I fay, and *maximè à crepitando & eruétando* ; that is, from emitting ventofities or flatuofities from his concavities : with feveral other admonitions, according to the diétates of *Joannes Sulpitius,* and *Guilielmus Lillius,* my two very good and learned friends————

Mar. Will he never make an end ?

Man. But, above all, Ladies, for refpeét to his friends (becaufe I am incarcerate with obligations to all his paternal Relations) I did alwayes exhort him to abftain from tripudiation or dauncing, gladiation or fencing, lufitation or gaming, equitation or riding, *& fic de cæteris* ; So that now he is one of the beft educate youths in *Florence,* elfe *Ego operam & oleam perdidi.*

Chryf. He is very much obliged to you, Sir.

Man. Now, I will not moleft you with a more ample relation of his good qualifications; but, he is a friend to modefty and chaftity, an enemy to fuperbity, *in potu moderatus* ; but, *notandum*———— he is moft locuplete both in argentary and frumentary rents———— not given to luxury or venery————no, not at at all to venery————

Mar. What a tedious harangue for nothing.

Man. But, (to conclude, becaufe now the time is gone) as I faid before, as I fay now, and I hope your intelligence does comprehend, when he comes into Town, I fhall concomitate him to your domicile

cile, diverfory, chamber, cubicular, or what you pleafe, and——fo
farewell. *Exit.*

Chryf. What a meer Pedant!

Mar. As ever liv'd, Sifter, I cannot love him.

Chryf. Peace, Sifter, let us appear civil before him; for, he is
imployed by that Gentelman *Becabunga's* friends, to found our
humours I warrand you——

And what our friends have ordain'd, we will do,

What e're it be, there's reafon for it too.

Exeunt.

Scæna Sexta.

Enter Arabella *fola, as at* Siena, *having got intelligence
of the Rebels victory.*

Ar.——Too true——I fear'd it alwayes;——now frail woman,
Has thou no eyes? Art thou not fenfible
Already of our flavery?——*Barbaro,*
A *Florentine,* a profef'd enemy
To all *Siennois,* will become our Mafter.
——But hold——imagine the brave *Marciano,*
As gods know, and I fear, a prifoner.
Confequently thy heart in quarter with him,
——Pray, what wouldft do? Refolve, poor *Arabella,*
Would'ft not go fearch him? or would'ft rather ftay
Thou at *Siena* here, he, God knows where.
Love prompts the firft, honour perfwades the laft,
This fear advifes, that hope ftrongly preffes;
Fear tells me, I fhould erre; for, may be he
Whom in profperity, I did fcarce efteem,
May now forget me too, (a fault our Sex
Ofttimes commit, more through infirmity
Then malice) yet, were I affur'd he were
Prifoner in *Florence,* I'd no more debate,
But fearch and find him, at whatever rate. *Exit.*

C 2 *Actus*

Actus Secundus. Scæna Prima.

Enter Marciano, *a boy with him as in an Inn.*

——THis Inn is good——now late——I might have here
Convenient lodging, if I durft but ftay——
——Sirrah, go fee my horfes——   *Exit Boy.*
                    A chair fet out.
Good gods ! is't come to this ?——muft we behold
Rebellion in its full *Epitafis ?*
No antidote to fave th'empoyfoned State ?——
——Thofe forces, I had rallyed, now undone,
Routed, quite routed——what fhall I refolve - ——
I've overcome a tedious voyage——O !
If I could now have but one half hours reft,
That with good news from my Prince would refrefh
Both body and foul——But yet how can my eyes
Receive their lawfull tribute, when my heart
Is tofs'd 'twixt hope and love ?——hope bids me live
To fee a bleffed *Cataftrophe* yet to all
Our prefent tumults——love perfwades me rather
To dye, then fee the vertuous *Arabella,*
(Although unkind to me, as yet defpifing
My ardent fuit) become a prey to fuch
As know no love, but in their tyranny.
O heavenly, divine creature——would thou know   *(fits down*
My prefent flames——wer't poffible thofe fighs
My troubled heart fends forth, might be condenf'd
Into one body :——fure they could inform
Thofe very ftones with breath, thofe ftones fhould move :
Thofe ftones fhould fpeak ; and as they are become
The only witneffes of my complaint,
So be the true Embaffadours of my forrow ;

To fhow the vertuous *Arabella*———that———
Thus———for———her love——— *takes a nap.*
Enter boy haftily.
My Lord———the enemy———the enemy———Fly...Fly...Fly.
Exit boy running

Marciano bolts out of his chair.
Fly! Fly! avaunt with that base cowardly gibbrifh ;
That *Algebra* of honour ; which had never
Been nam'd, if all had equal courage———what ?
I fly ! Poor rogue, 'had as good bid me dye. *(draws*
I'le force my way, or make a noble end,
Valour does fometimes humane wit tranfcend.
Enter Souldiers, fwords drawn, &c.
1. *Soul.* This way———'tis he———take quarter.
Marc. Quarter ! ———no flaves———I'le fee your entrails firft.
Thus Dogs——— }*fight, Sould. falls back,*
  Marciano purfues.

Enter again haftily.
The hounds are now at a bay———
———No way t'efcape———fortune, if not me,
Commiferate at leaft my Prince———I prize not
My life, if I muft dye, transform my foul
Into fome loyal breaft,———I dye contented.
Enter Soul. as before.
There again———villains, are you fo bold
———'This fword fhall tame you——— }*falls back as before,*
  Marciano purfues.

A noyfe within. Enter Borafco, *Souldiers with them,*
Marciano prifoner.
Bor. Sir, your noble courage hath oblidged our care,
The tearms of your furrender fhall be obferved
Faithfully———now to horfe———
Marc. I do obey, Sir, for with fuch as you
A word does more, then oaths with cowards do.
Exeunt omnes.

Scæna

Scæna Secunda.

Enter Manduco, *with* Signior Becabunga, *knock at the door,* &c.

Man. Ho ——who is within there ?   } *Enter Boy.*
  Boy. Your fervant Gentlemen.
Man. Is the Lady *Marionetta* within ?
Boy. Yes, Sir, Pray what are you, who demands ?
Man. Why, here is Signior *Becabunga* newly come to town——
But heark you, is fhe occupyed ?
Boy. How Sir.
Man. Profane Fellow——I mean, is fhe not busie——that is to
fay, at leifure ?
Boy. O, yes——pleafe you walk in.
Man. Yes——yes——heus———*ingrediamur.*

                                                        Exeunt.
       Enter again at the other end, chairs Jet.
  Boy. Pleafe you to walk here a little, while I go call the
Ladies.   *Exit.*
  Man. Remember now, when you are in private to propone
matrimony with a great deal of ceremony, and for your comple-
ments, you may call her the Lady that triumphs in the Coach-box
of your affections, a bewitching *Syren,* a beautifull *Thais,* and fo
forth, as occafion offers.   Praife her hair, her eyes, her ears, her
breafts, &c.   There is abundance of choice epithetes to be had, you
may say her face is like a Print-book of divers characters, that puzles
the reader, her nofe like the ftyle of a Dyal, her eyes like Stars, her
hair like Gold, her teeth like Ivory, her veins like filk, and her breafts
like milk, and fo forth, as I faid before :——you'l remember on
this now.
  Bec. Yes, yes, I warrand you, I fhall remember——let me fee
now, her breafts, her fhoulders, her toes, her fingers, her nayls
and her nofe———But hark you, muft I say nothing of her
cloaths ?

                                                          Man.

Man. How come you to say that now?

Bec. Why? her nofe makes me remember on it.

Man. ——So——fo—come fall upon the ⎱ *Enter* Chryfolina, Mari-
Ladyes——go——I fay.   ⎰ onetta, Bec. *Salutes, &c.*

Bec. Ladyes, I am indeed glad to fee you now.

Man. Ladyes, I am your devotionated devotionary.

Mar. You are welcome to Town Sir.

Bec. Proteft, Ladyes, I am your humble fervant.

Man. As before, *nam cælum non animum mutat.* ⎱ Man. *prompts*
Bec. As before, *nam cælos non animus mutat.* ⎰ *him behind his back.*

Man. You are wrong—Say——I did long vehemently to fee you
——as one in child-bed.

Bec. I did long vehemently to see you in child-bed.

Man. A meer brutum animall!   ⎱ Man. *retires in*
Bec. What's the matter, Sir, did not I fay ⎰ *a rage* Becabunga
very well now.   *followes him.*

Man. No——it was altogether finiftruous, I have effodiate
the treafure of my brain in educating you,——and yet for all that
you are a meer *ignoramus.*

Bec. O——I will do well enough yet——Pray, tell me what I
fhould say, for the Ladyes are waitting upon me.

Man. No——I will complement them my felf——fpeak not you
——*ne vel unum gru.*

Ladyes, This gentelman is newly arrived at *Florence* the defuetude
of amorous converfation, with the affuetude of rurall exercifes
have fo, as I may fay, confounded his intellectuals, that if he hefi-
tate in the pronunciation, he hopes you will meerly attribute it to
his campeftriall, trimeftriall perigrination.

Chryf. We not only excufe you, Sir, but likewife account our-
felves honoured by your vifit——Pray fit down Sir.

Man. Yes, yes, without ceremony.   ⎱ Bec. *fits down by*
Bec. Why——I think, you are filent, Madam. ⎰ Mar Man. *fits betwixt the Ladyes.*

Mar. I love not to prate Sir.

Bec. Nor I either.

Man. Nay so long as he was under my *ferula*; I did labour to
coerce in him that loquacious verbofity, or rather verbofious lo-
quacity

quacity, with which moſt part of the perverſe temporary adoleſ-
cency is contaminate, for I hate garrulity, as I am facundious,
I do.

Bec. I vow, Madam, you are very bony, ſince I) Man. *takes a*
fee you laſt——O, I have had rare paſtime in the) *pype of tobacco.*
country this harveſt, brave hunting, and hawking of hares ; and
but the laſt day comming in to the Town, I tooke a couple of them
by the way. O, Madam, you will not beleeve what brave ſport
wee have now. I wonder why you have ſtay'd in city all this
while ?

Mar. What ſhould we have done in the country, Sir, hunted,
and hawked as you doe?

Man. I hope this does not offend you, Madam. *Chryſ.* Not
at all, Sir.

Man. I ſhould be loath to offend any) *Smoakes in Chryſ. face*
man, but I am without ceremony.) *Smoakes in Mar. face.*

Mar. Uſe your own liberty, Sir,

Man. Nay, I do it to draw down reuthm from my brain, with
which my lungs are much infeſted : for, d'you ſee, 'tis a very ſalu-
tiferous herbe : it diſpoſes the minde for ſtudy, and moves in ſeve-
rall places ; I will ſhow you what by it's help I made laſt night ;
marry a ſonnet upon a Lady, whoſe beauty had almoſt tempted me
to affect her.——*She walk'd*) ſings. Nay ; hold, I have a good
voice for writing, but not for reading. I will read then.

Sonnet

She walk'd along with ſuch a grace,
And ſuch a catching eye,
That, had her Maſque not hid her face
Then——certainly——
In ſome degree,
I had become a lover certainly.

I had become
Both blind, and dumb,
For Cupids thundring dart
Had pierc'd my heart.
It had——by my facunditie.

But

But I more prudent was then fo
  Affoon as fhe drew nigh
I turn'd my back to her, and lo
  She glyded by.
  Immediatly.
Then I began to ruminate, and fay
  What is wo——man ?
  Even no——man.
Why then fhould wee love her,
  Seing we are above her,
And fhe, at beft, mans hacqueney ?

Man. arifes.

——But heark you, Madam, I beleeve 'tis now time wee fhou'd leave them to their private confabulation.

Chryf. Yes Sir, with all my heart.

Man. One word then with this Gentelman, and I am gone——
Heus, be attentive and circumfpectious in your behaviour, remember on thofe *elegantes phrafes,* I taught you when you came in : fo I will retire, and leave you for a fpace.

Exit with Chryf.

Bec. Now wee are all alone, Madam, I hope you know my errand.

Mar. Not well, Sir.

Bec. I am fure, my 'Father faid he caufed the Lady *Saromanca* fpeak to you, or elfe I am deceived.

Mar. But you had beft fpeak to my Uncle, Sir ; I am at hi⸴ difpofall.

Bec. You are very modeft.   ⸾*Offers to kiffe, fhe refufes*

Mar. And I hope that is a vertue in a maid, Sir.

Bec. As I am a virgin, it is ; I love you all the better for it and I'le affure you fo long as you are modeft, you can never be impudent.   *Enter Boy.*

Madam, *Signior Pantaloni* is below, fhall I tell him you are within ?

Mar. Yes, yes, by all means, you muft not deny us to fuch a Gentelman of quality as he is.

Bec. Signior Pantaloni, fay you, my old comrade, I would be very glad to fee him.

D   *Mar*

Mar. He is in fuite of my Sifter, a Gentelman of a great eftate. I am much for the match ; I'le go caufe my Sifter come hither.

At the other end enter Signior Pantaloni, *Bec. falutes him.*

Bec. Signior Pantaloni !

Pant. Signior Becabunga——welcome to Town in good faith—— Yow are very gallant. ⟩*Surveyes Bec. cloaths.*

Bec. ——It is my winter fuite, Sir, it coft my Father a good deal of money, more than the price of ten bolls of wheat, or barley, I warrand you.

Pant. I am fure, you have had brave fport in the country all this while.

Bec. O yes : you know my dog *Springo* ?

Pant. Yes, and *Gafto, graybitcho, brounhoundo,* and all the tribe of them : I knew them all fince they were puppets, and your felf too.

Bec. Why, I will let him loofe with any 'his match in *Tufcany.*

Pant. O what a fool was I, might not I have been with you all this while, if it had not been for this baggagely Miftris of mine, Madam *Chryfolina,* call you her, whom my Mother will have me to woo whether I will or not, I may fay ; I had been in the country all this harveft.——But, what fhall I tell you, have not I learn'd fince I fee you to dance forsooth——that's a *coupee*— ⟩*frifks about.* that's a *circumflex pas :* that's a *tranfverfe pas, &c.,* ⟩

Bec. O brave *Pantaloni !* ⟩*Enter* Manduco *leading the Ladyes.*

Pant. I, but I can fence too—*zeeft—zeeft—zeeft* ⟩*Thrufts at Bec.*

Pant. Ladyes, I hope I have not com'd in into you ⟩ *Difcover* as I may fay intrufioufly, or intrufively. ⟩ *the Ladyes.*

Chryf. Not at all Sir, you are very welcome, pray how does your Lady mother, and your Sifters ?

Pant. All in good health, Madam, at your fervice——*Signior Manduco,* you are welcome to Town.

Man. Signior Pantaloni, I am yours integrally, and *quafi exulto* in the profperity of this our congreffion.

Enter Boy.

Madam, the two Gentelmen you call *Cafio and Leonardo* defire to fee you.

Mar.

Mar. Go tell them we are not within.

Chryſ. Tell them we are not at leaſure, Sirrah.

Exit Boy.

Man. What are they ?

Pant. Ranting, young blades, like the times, I warrand you, two fellows, that have frequented all your Stage-playes in *Italy*, and I heard our Chaplain ſay ; and my Siſter too (which is more) that Playes were very unlawfull and impious.——

Man. Playes are indeed profane, ſcelerate, abominable, yea, abominably abominable——which I will maintain *multis argumentis.*

Pant. Beſides, they are great mockers of ſuch Gentlemen as us, who are better then themſelves.

Man. Are they of the Dukes party ?

Pant. Yes, I warrand you.

Man. *Hoc ſatis eſt*——*odi totam gentem* : Ladies, you do well not to converſe with them——but no more of them : Ladies, what would you think of a perambulation in this calid, æſtivous ſeaſon ?

Chryſ. But whether ſhall we walk, Sir ?

Pant. Any where, Madam, I ſhall wait upon you.

Bec. And, I ſhall ſtick cloſe to my Lady, forſooth.

Mar. Wee'l have a coach then.

Bec. By all means——call a Coach.

within, Coach, &c.

Man. Let us then paſſe the Pomeridian hours in obambulation : for I am defatigate with ſeſſion.

Exeunt omnes.

*D*₂   *Scæna*

Scæna Tertia.

Enter Borafco *with* Arabella *Prifoner.*

Ar. GOod my Lord, for the refpect to honour,
Prove courteous to a poor diftreffed Lady,
And now your prifoner——
  Bor. My prifoner——Not, by this hand, fo much,
As I am yours.   (*kiffes her hand.*
  Ar. I fhould belye my paffion, Sir, if I,
Next to the publike deftiny of my Country,
Did not refent my own calamity ;
But yet your undeferved clemency
Does moderate my misfortunes——
  Bor. How ! undeferved——when even *Cannibals*,
Tam'd by the afpect of your radiant eye,
Would quit their barb'rous, fuperftitious rites,
And offer, what their gods ufurp, to you.
  Ar. Sir, I owe much, I muft confefs, to nature,
But your applaufe inflames the bill more high,
'Tis now our common fate to be imprifon'd,
But not fo common to be thus refpected.
  Bor. Lady, what the Lord *Barbaro* hath ordain'd
I hold it always juftice——but becaufe
Your face does fpeak you one, whom all fhould honour,
That e're have known what love is, I regrate
This your confinement ; the caufes of which
Are only known to his excellency,   (*Enter Iaylor.*
Time will difcover all——but here he comes
Who muft be your guardian——Sirrah——
  Jayl. Your pleafure, my Lord ?
  Bor. By order from the Senate, you'r commanded
To take this Lady in your cuftody——
See you refpect her, Sirrah,——let her not

Be

Be uf'd, as other ordinary prisoners.
Mark what I say, you varlet——serve her well.

Jayl. I shall, forsooth, my Lord, she shall be as well uf'd as
any Lady can be in prison.

Bor. Madam, I'le visit you sometimes, and see
You treated, like an honourable Lady.
This Fellow shall have special care of you,
Command him at all times ; and for my service,
Pray spare it not——farewell——she is my prisoner,   (*aside.*
I shall have fit time yet t'impart my flames.

Exit.

Jayl. Now, forsooth, Madam, will you be pleased to walk——
I'le conduct you to as neat, a wel-swipp'd, wel-trimm'd Room,
as you can have in many parts of *Florence* : My Lord *Borasco*,
is a very obliging Gentleman, and I'le assure you, he loves to be
courteous ; I will have a care of you for his sake ; my Wife, and
I (I must have you acquaint with her, Madam) for she is one of the
loving'st, dutifull, old Sluts, that you have known——

Ar. Come then, let's go——

Jayl.——My Wife and I, I say, Madam, shall serve you to a
hair, for she loves to be courteous, as well as my self.

Ar. Where are my Countrymen lodg'd ?   I'd rather
Be with them, as elsewhere——

Jayl. A *Pisan*, Madam ?

Ar. No——a *Siennois.*

[*Jayl.*] There are many *Siennois* Nobles in my custody.

Ar. The Lord *Marciano* : since 'tis my misfortune
To be his Fellow-prisoner.

Jayl. Madam, you shall see him, for I love to be courteous,
especially to strangers, Madam.

Exeunt.

Scæna.

Scæna Quarta.

Enter Chryſolina, Marionetta, *as in their Chamber.*

Mar. How did you like our laſt entertainment, Siſter?
    Chryſ. Indifferently well; I love that ſame Gentleman, *Signior Becabunga*: he is none of your ranting young Gallants, but a ſober youth as is in all *Florence.*

Mar. 'Tis true, but yet——

Chryſ. —What——don't you love him, Siſter? you are a fool if you let ſuch a fair occaſion ſlip——ſuch a fine Woodcock is not ſtart every day :——he hath a great Eſtate, Siſter, remember that.

Mar. 'Tis all true——

Chryſ. I, and he will not readily ſpend it; his Tutor, *Manduco,* hath bred him very ſparingly——honeſt man, I proteſt he is an honeſt man :——yea, a very honeſt man.

Mar. He is indeed——

Chryſ. And then, Siſter, you may have a very contented life with him : he is a good-natur'd, ſweet youth, he will give you all your will, and I'l aſſure you that is a great property in a man.

Mar. ——And what think you of your own Suitor, *Pantaloni* all this while?

Chryſ. Why——I know not what I ſhall ſay of him yet.

Mar. Goodneſs ! how came they here?

Leon. Nay, my pretty *Daphne,* fly not my embraces, I know we have ſurpriſ'd you now.

> } *Enter* Caſsio, Leonardo, *quietly.*
> } *Mar. diſcovers them.*
> } Chryſ. *ſtarts back.*
> } *amazed.*

Caſſ. What pretty intrigue of love was the objeſt of your diſcourſe, pray let us be ſharers with you in your entertainment.

Leon. My life for't, you were deviſing ſome ſtratagem, how to croſſe the deſigns of ſome affeſtionat Votary : you have no pity on our Sex now a dayes, Ladies.

Caſſ. None, indeed, if you were not viſible in this age, then we ſhould not love : but, when we once conceive flames of affeſtion

for

tor you, in lieu of fomenting us in our delights, you make love a difeafe to us by your unmercifull nicety, which deprives us; altogether of your converfation : this is fad, Ladies ; truft me 'tis fad.

Mar. You wrong our Sex, Sir.

Chryf. But, d'you hear, Sir, ferioufly I intreat you would forbear fuch vifits ; for, you will but give people occafion to talk of what we never thought on.

Mar. And befides, Sir, thofe who challenge power over us will be offended at this entertainment : we intreat you then, Gentlemen, to leave us.

Caff. Farewell, then, cruel beauty, but do not imagine fuch a harfh repulfe will ftop the current of my boundlefs love ; abfence fhall never prove fo fatal : but while my breath fhall demonftrate that I live, this heart, this fpeech and this hand fhall demonstrate that I love you. Farewell bright ftar of my fancy. } *to* Mar.

Exit.

Leon. Such a fair Lady cannot be fo cruel, I will not take this anfwer as a repulfe, but rather conftrue it the moft favourable way. Farewell, time, I hope, fhall melt the feverity of your refolutions. } *to* Chryf.

Exit.

Chryf. Farewell my ranting gamfters, we are not meat for your mouths.——What foolifh people have we in our houfe, Sifter, to admit them Gentlemen ?——why, they came in upon us while we were ferious.

Mar. Yes, Sifter, and if one of us had been commenting on the Pifs-pot, it had been all one to them, when doors are left open.

Chryf. And knowing that our friends cannot endure them, they fhould, at leaft, in confcience, have denied them accefs. O ! how I fhall baffle them fame wenches that did not look to our Chamber door better.

Mar. I proteft, Sifter, we must marry quickly, otherwayes we fhall be conftantly infefted with fuch importunate Suitors ; and that, in my opinion, is no great pleafure to a woman, it diftracts their fpirits, me thinks.

Chryf.

Chryf. You fay right, Sifter, wee fhall never be well, untill we be even well marryed.

Exeunt.

Scæna Quinta.

Enter Borafco, *with* Arabella *in prifon.*

Bor. **L** Ady, I have at length obtain'd that favour
Of the Lord *Barbara*, you may go abroad
To any part o'th citty that you pleafe.
Providing you return hither at night———
Ar. My Lord, I thank you kindly. I find you have
Exceeded in your favours, fince I came
Into this prifon : you have (without flattery)
Even overacted courtefie to me———
Bor. I plead not fo for every one, but you
May challenge my refpects :———the power I have
As captain of the Guards, fhall be employed
To ferve you, Madam, as you pleafe command me.
Ar. Then 'pray, my Lord, 'mongst others, grant me this,
To fee the Lord *Marciano.*
Bor. Madam, I fhall conduct you to his Chamber,
Or, if you pleafe, he fhall come hither to you.
Ar No, I will go to him.

Exeunt.

Scæna Sixta.

At the other end enter Marciano, *with him the* Jaylor.

Mar. **A** Lady, fay'ft thou ?
Jayl. Yes, my Lord, a young Lady.
Marc. A Lady, and a *Siennois,*——ftrange!

Who

Who can this be !——but now I have a thought,
Yet I dare not expreffe it——can it be !
No, fure——impoffible——prethee begone,
And leave me to my felf——

Jayl. She will be here by and by, my Lord.   *Exit Jayl.*

                        Marciano folus.

Marc. Well, who this Lady is, I cannot think,
But in a dreame :——O, may I yet imagine,
"Tis fhe——Nay, hold —— my hope cannot support } *Enter Arabella*
Such a ftrong thought of bleffe ! I fhall offend   } *quietly.*
Even in thinking——   } *Marciano difcovers her.*
——A cheat——a meer cheat——eyes do not gull me.
The Lady *Arabella* !——No, unleffe
I heare her talk,——I'l think it ftill a phantafme } *Approaches*
——Speak fair ghoft——is it thee ?   } *to her.*

Ar. *Marciano,* it is I, the unfortunate *Arabella.*

Marc. Then it is no more I——O——how I am } *Embraces h r.*
Tranfported ! how that divine voyce hath ravifhed
My duller fenfes !——is't poffible, you weep
In fympathy with my afflictions ?

Ar. Yea altogether.

Marc. Good gods ! it is fhe-——O does *Arabella,* } *Embraces*
Who, while I was in full profperity,   } *again.*
Did frown upon my Paffions : ftoop fo low,
As fee me now in mifery——unleffe
She mean, as children, with their hobby-horfes,
T'unravell me, that fhe may thereby fee
What ftuff I do contain :——dare I prefume
To think that love to me hath brought you hither ?

Ar. Moft true——nought elfe——

Marc. Fair innocence, whofe prefence does revive
My fpirits in this agony of forrowes,
While I am coop'd up, as a parrot, here,
Expecting every day, when *Atropos*
Shall cut my thread of life; that thou fhould daigne
To vifit me ! had your fair hand difpatch'd
One word in poft, it had been too great honour.

                    E   But

But thus to be thy own Embaſſadour,
'Tis a bewitching happineſſe ; no tongue
Can well expreſſe my paſſion——good, my ſtars
Preferve me from an extaſie !——
   Ar. You wrong me, *Marciano*, I left *Siena*,
Hearing of your bad ſucceſſe ; thence I came
To *Luca* ; there not finding you, to *Florence*,
To ſee if I could purchaſe your enlargement,
Either by art, or favour : but no ſooner
Was I come hither, when I was ſuſpected
As one, who keep't ſecret intelligence
With the Dukes party here, and ſo committed——
   Marc.——Committed—how !—committd—heathniſh wretches !
Barbarous Rebells ! to impriſon one,
Whom Indians had ſpar'd,——By *Mars*——unheard of
Even amongſt *Turks*, and *Tartars* ! *Ar.* Nay forbear,
I am not ſo unfortunate, as you think,   •
The Senate meaning thus to puniſh me
Have rather cheriſh'd me :——your company
May well allay my griefs.
   Marc. By this ——and this——   }*Kiſſes her hand.*
You honour me too much, but which is ſad,
I never ſhall be able to repay
That love to you, which I owe, ſeing every hour
I doe expect my ſentence——
   Ar. Alas ! harſh fates ! O frail reward of courage !
                         Enter Jaylor.
   Jayl. Madam, my duty bears me to conduct you to your
Chamber, it is now high time.
   Ar. My Lord, adieu, I ſhall ſee you to morrow.
               Marciano ſolus.   *Exit with Jayl.*
   Marc. Farewell, my ſouls delight,—O unkind Stars !
A fit theatre for ſuch entertainment !
An embleme of our love !——But I exclaim
Unſeaſonably.——O how prettily
Fortune hath tyed me, as a Shrove-tide bird,
While *Saturne*, *Mars* and *Cupid* levell at me :

                                    ——A

——A fig for all her tricks——·I fcorn her frown,
She can win nothing, while my hearts my own.   *Exit.*

Scæna Septima.

Enter Strenuo *with the* Jaylor.

Stren. IS he fentenced already?
    Jayl. No, got yet; but he muſt die.
  Stren. Well——let him go, 'twill learn others to be wife, friend;
for, Souldiers haue but fhrewd arrears paid them now for their
fervice.

Jayl. I am really forry for him; as I am true *Florentine* he is
a noble Gentelman, and loves to be courteous——

Stren. But, d'you hear, Mr. Jaylor, fhall we have t'other cup
the night?

Jayl. I——at the *Siena* Tavern, *Signior Strenuo,* where we
may have a cup of good Canary; I am for you there, *Signior Strenuo,* and will fpend my checquin moſt heartily, *Signior* ; for, I love
to be frolique as well as courteous, efpecially with ſtrangers, *Signior.*

Stren. ——Come then, brave old Boy, we'll have a cup o'th beſt
on't. Will you go along now and I'l give you your morning
draught?

Jayl. No——not now; I muſt wait upon my Lord *Borafco,*
he fent word that he would be here by and by.

Stren. Farewell then——at night——old *Hary*——at night.
                                   Exit Stren.

Jayl. Yes, yes, I fhall not fail you *Signior,* I warrand you. This
fame *Strenuo* is a notable fellow, as ever I knew of a *Siennois* : he
loves to be courteous, effaith.

          Enter Borafco *with Souldiers.*

Bor. See it be done, I fay, the Senate means
To whip moſt of your ſtubborn *Siennois,*
By his example——firrah, Jaylor. *Jayl.* My Lord.

Bor. The Lord *Marciano* is condemn'd to die——
Jayl. The time, my Lord——
                  E 2   *Bor.*

Bor. Within fix dayes, no more refpite——
Here are the Generals orders for it.
——Sirrah, look to your prifoner, watch him well.
I'l double all the ordinary guards
About the prifon ; place my Sentinels
In every corner——
    Jayl. I fhall watch him, my Lord, I'l affure you,
    Bor. As you will anfwer us : now he fhall die.
       Although he hath efcap'd fometimes before,
       His worfhip fhall play faft and loofe no more.

                            Exeunt omnes.

Scæna Octava.

Enter Chryfolina, Marionetta, *as in their Chamber.*

Chryf. I Profefs ingenuoufly, Sifter, I am afhamed of it.
      Mar. And I likewife ; for people give eafily credit to
any report now a dayes.
    Mar. Let's rather be uncivil as admit them next time, Sifter :
I love no fuch company, I'l affure you.
               Enter Signior Pantaloni.
    Pant. Ladies, I am come to wait upon you again——according
to my duty——as in duty I am bound to undertake.
    Chryf. Sir, you are very welcome, I hope your mother is well.
    Pant. Yes, forfooth, Madam, how does your felf ?
    Chryf. In very good health, Sir, I thank you.
    Pant. I am very glad——But, hark you, Madam——one word
in private with you—— }*to Mar.* This by your leave Miftris.   }*leads her aside.*
    Hark you me now——my mother and I were fitting by the
fire-fide laft night, as it is our cuftom, you know, in the winter-
nights after fupper ; and——I do not know what we were talking
of : but, amongft the reft I remember, if I have not forgot,——
that fhe faid——fhe said, fayes fhe——Now——whether this
                                          be

be true or not, I cannot tell; you know beft yourfelf: but, I am fure fhe faid it.

Chryf. What, pray Sir?

Pant. Now——I vow——if it were true, I would be as glad of it, as ever I was of my break-faft in a cold day;——for, I proteft ingenuoufly, I am fure you know, I love to be ferious.

Chryf. Pray what's the matter, Sir?

Pant. Why——I vow I know you would blufh now, elfe I would tell you it.

Chryf. I befeech you refolve me, Sir.

Pant. I vow, I can hardly do it now, I am fo ftupi- } *kiffes her* fied——with the rarity of the object of your perfon. } *hand.*

Chryf. I can have no longer patience——

Pan. ——Nay, hold——here's it now——I hope you will not tell it again; for it was told me as a great fecret——why fayes fhe - ——but, as I told you, I know not furely if it be true or not: but, fhall I tell you what I anfwered——Marry, Lady mother, fayes I——I fear you are but fcorning me.

Chryf. But, what was it that fhe faid, Sir?

Pant. Why——I vow——fhe——even faid——that——you loved me——and O but I was blyth——

Chryf. Hum——and is that all? keep fuch a long difcourfe for nothing.

Pant. O!——I hope you are not angry.

Chryf. No, no, Sir.

Mar. Why——you might have faid all that in three words, Sir.

Pant. Nay——but prethee tell me if it be true: for, if it be not, I fhall win two Ryals from my mother: for, fhe and I laid a wager upon it, and I am come here for nothing elfe but to be refolved of it.

Mar. Well——then, you have win, Sir.

Pant. Nay——do not mock me now; I profefs, I had rather lofe a dozen of Ryals before fhe fhould not love me: for, I am fure——as fure as this glove is upon my hand——I love her.

Enter Boy.

Boy. Madam, dinner is ready.

Chryf. We come. *Signior,* will you dine with us, and——afterwards we fhall talk of that at more leafure. *Pant.*

Pant. With all my heart, fair Ladyes, If you pleafe, I will fup with you, and lye with you too——I love your company fo well.   *Exeuut omnes.*

Actus Tertius, Scæna Prima.

Arabella fola appears fitting at a table as in her Chamber, &c.

Ar. L Oaden with cares : o'rewhelm'd with misfortunes !
      Can female fhoulders bear my heavie croffes——
I left my native country of *Siena*.
To find out *Marciano* here at *Florence* :
Now have I found him : but O ! how, God knowes,
And I too well percieve :——unhumane fates,
Whether, ah ! whether will you hurrie me ?
No end to your feverity :——Ay me !
What have I done ? pray let me know my crime : ,
As yet I plead ftrong innocence : unleffe
It be a crime to love : pray fhow my faults,
Or elfe fufpend my paines——
Now (which is fad) I can fcarce have repofe
For fighs and cares : and when I once awake
Borufco, therein my true *Jaylor,* waits me,
With frefh follicitations :——thus my heart
Is rent in peeces ; th'one half forrow claimes,
The other love——Ay me ! what fhall I do ?   ⎰ *weeps*

                              Enter Strenuo
  Str. Shee's difcontent already : but thofe newes
I bring, will make her fadder : I dare fcarce
Declare them, leaft fhe fwoon——Madam.
  Ar. Welcome, dear *Strenuo,* pray how does thy Lord ?
  Str. Well, Madam,——but e're long, if fates prevent not——
  Ar. How—that again,——me thinks, thou looks not chearfull
As thou were wont,——how does my Lord, I fay ?

                                                                Str.

Str. (If I dare tell you) he's condemn'd to dye.

Ar. ——To dye !——Ay me——be mercifull, and kill me
Good *Strenuo,* honeft friend———prethee difpatch——

Str. Stay madam, you are mad——

Ar. —Condemn'd to dye——
O how my heart ftrings, by that pin of grief,
As by an unexpert muficians hand,
Who ftrives to raife his Lute to higheft notes,
Tun'd up above the nick begin to crack.

Str. Forbear, fair Lady, 'tis no time to weep,
Now wee muft doo; now wee muft mufter all
Our wits to plot his efcape——

Ar. As how——Alas fond *Strenuo* :——efcape !
Dream not on that, rather invent fome meanes,
How wee may dye together, like true lovers.

Str. Madam, you wrong your felf, I'le undertake.
By your affiftance, to effect my purpofe.

Ar. By my affiftance, prethee doubt not that,
What will I not do, if I can, to fave him ?

Str. Then, Madam, here is *aquafortis* for you.
Look——this will do it, Lady, this applyed
To th'iron grate o'th window, will confume it
In a fhort fpace ; then in the filent night
By help of a fmall rope he may efcape.

Ar. 'Tis well, but all depends on th'*aquafortis,*
I cannot fafely carry it to his chamber ;
That *Cerberus,* that ugly cat-ey'd *Jaylor*
Will fure difcover me——

Str. Nay, as for him,
I'le keep the villain tipling all the while
He never fhall fufpect you ; I've provided
A fouldiers habit for my Lord, in which garb
The devill himfelf fhall never fmell him out.
I'le fo difguife him :——go good Madam, go
Tender my love to him, and preffe him by
All meanes to ufe it quickly I'le wait on him

At

At th'hour appointed——
  Ar. I go, pray heavens, it may fucceed.
  Str. Fear not.   *Exeunt feverally.*

Scæna Secunda.

Enter Caffio *and* Leonardo.

Caff. SO——you intend thither again, *Leonardo*, you were high-
ly entertained, Boy.
  Leon. And I believe, *Caffio*, you had but fmall encouragement.
  Caff. Small encouragement indeed; bnt you muft know, love is
never in it's height, fo long as limitate within the fphere of reafon;
I love her fo much the more that fhe appears unreafonable, as you
call it.
  Leon. But, afide, here comes *Don Quixot* ⎱ *Enter* Becabunga *and*
and *Sancho Pancho.*   ⎰ Pantaloni *difcourfing.*
  Caff. 'Slid, let's accoft them.
  Leon. No, let's firft obferve their behaviour.
  Pant. Say you fo; O! I long furioufly to travel.
  Bec. I mar'le you delay fo long.
  Pant. Why, I vow my trunk hath been twice a fhip-board for
Marfeilles, and myfelf at *Ligorn,* but, I vow my mother weep'd
fo, that I could not find in my heart to leave her.
  Bec. And it may be the Lady *Chryfolina* would not permit you.
  Pant. O——no; I know fhe would wait upon me fome half
year, or fo yet while I faw *France* and came back again; although
I vow, fhee's a pretty, pretty, pretty Gentlewoman, as I know be-
twixt me and her.
  Bec. You will have her yet, I warrand you.
  Pant. I hope fo; for I am fure fhe loves me, or elfe I have no
skill.
  Bec. Does fhe fo, and that is fome encouragement though.
  Caff. Prethee let's interrupt them, enough of fuch difcourfe in
all confcience.
  Leon. Yes, now we will accoft them———Gentlemen, the
                                          general

general character of you in this City, hath rendred us ambitious of your acquaintance.

Caſſ. Signior *Becabunga,* you are moſt auſpiciouſly returned to the City.

Bec. Your humble ſervant, Sir ; your *extollation* of me is undeſerved.

Leon. Sir, I do but what all ingenuous perſons } *Leon* to *Pant.* ſhould do, no queſtion you are conſcious of your } Caſſ. *takes* Bec. own merits. } *aſide.*

Pant. Sir, the faculty of my expreſsion————is not capable to entertain——as I may ſay————or expreſs the motion of my affeſtion, to uphold——as I may ſay, acquaintance, familiarity with you——I hope you underſtand me, Sir.

Leon. Yes, and admires your wit too, Sir.

Pant. Sir, I am your very humble ſervant ; I hope I need not back it with an oath ; *nam, nemo tenetur* (you know) *jurare in ſuum detrimentum.*

Caſſ. Good, and what ſaid they ?

Bec. Why, they ſaid you were a couple of idle youths.

Leon. How !——*Caſſ.* Prethee let me hear out this diſcourſe.

Pant. ——Ho, ho, very true, I proteſt I think they wrong'd you : for, for my own part, as I am Gentleman, I think you are very civil, although I ſay it in your face.

Caſſ. Good, and no more prethee ?

Bec, Nay, now I have not leaſure, *Manduco* will be ſeeking me through all the Town ; O he will chide me, *if he find me not.*

Caſſ. Hang him a Loggar-head.

Bec. A Loggar-head, I would not for never ſo much he heard you ſay that ; he thinks himſelf no ſmall man I'l aſſure you.

Adieu, Sir————*Pantaloni,* will you go ?   *Exit Bec.*

Pant. Annon, Sir————Gentlemen, I ſhall be very willing and deſirous that we may entertain our preſent converſation willingly : and, for my part, *I have the honour* to drink one cup of wine with you, I will wait upon you at any time or place convenient, if there be no *lawfull impediment why theſe parties may not be joyn'd*————Oh, I crave you pardon, Gentlemen,————*Lapſus linguæ non eſt atramentum.* Farewell.   *Exit.*

Leon. Now, go thy wayes, *Signior Pantaloni*, thou art this day as compleat a *gull* as lives in *Florence*, *without difparagement of any Gentleman whatfoever.*

Caff. He hath difcovered all to me, *Leonardo*, I never read of fuch humorous Ladies.

Leon. And they will be fo alwayes, while we can render them gulls defpicable in their fight.

Caff. Let's think then how to affront them.

Leon. I'l rack my invention, but I will fet them by the ears together.

Caff. That were good, if you can do it handfomly.

Leon. I'l do my beft; come——let's go confult upon it.

Exeunt.

Scæna Tertia.

Enter Marciano, Arabella.

Marc. PErfwade me not, I cannot but abhor
　　　Such a prepofterous attempt——

Ar. My Lord——

Marc. Dear foul of fweetnefs, do not torture me
With fruitlefs plots——within four dayes I die——
Should I efcape and leave you prifoner——
——Think, think on that——

Ar. You may efcape, my Lord;
I have brought hither t'you, fome *aquafortis*
Which your friend *Strenuo* gave me this morning;
You may apply it to the grate o'th'window——

Marc. And what then——

Ar. Your friend affures me 'hath a Souldiers habit
In readinefs for you. This fame *aquafortis*
Will do the bufinefs——quick, apply it quickly——
Look to your felf, now it grows late, my Lord.

Marc. May I truft this——

Ar. You may, indeed, 'tis true.

Now

Now, now, or never, you muſt ſoon apply it——
This night you may as eaſily eſcape
  Marc. I'le try this trick for once.——
  Ar. Fear not the Jaylor ; he is fox'd already,
So *Strenuo* did aſſure me——
Apply it then, and if you don't eſcape——
Marc. I'le undertake it then——leave this with me,
I'le go about it preſently——mean time,
I'le cauſe put all in order——you muſt return
Within an hour hence :——and cauſe *Strenuo*
Be ready at the window——
  Ar. Fear not that.
  Marc. Farewell then.
  Ar. May my choyceſt prayers aſſiſt you.

                             Exit Marciano

                Arabella *ſola.*
  And if this fail, what can a womans wit
Invent, that will ſucceed ?——Alas, I fear,
Stil, ſtill, I fear, while he be ſafely hence.
I have uſ'd all means, nothing left untry'd
For his enlargement ; yet could not prevail.
——O love !——who can define thee——hopes and cares,
In conſtant ballance ; hov'ring up and down——
Here's a poor heart, within this troubled breaſt ;
That like a malefactor at the bar,
Trembles at this deſign :——O powerfull love——
What haſt thou not perſwaded me to do——

                        Sings behind the arras.
——But heark, a ſong, I will give ear to it,
I know *Boraſco* hath ordain'd it for me——
                Song.
                 I.
              So, ſo,
Lo Lillies *fade, before the* Roſes *ſhow*
Themſelves in bow-dye, ſummers-livery.
    Feaſting the curious eye,
    With choyce variety,
      F 2   *While*

While as before
We did adore
　　　Narciſſus *in his prime.*
Now Roſes do delyte
The nycer appetite :
Such is the vaſt diſparity of time.
　　　　　　2
　　　So, ſo,
One woman fades, before another know
What 'tis to be in love ; but in a trice
All men do ſacrifice
To th'latter, and deſpiſe
　　Her, whom before
　　They did adore
　　　Like Lillies *in their* prime.
　　Since now her ſparkling eyes
　　Are darkned in diſguiſe :
Such is the ſad diſparity of time.

Ar. A proper *ſimile*——now I ſee in what
Article *his pulſe* beats :——no *Syren* ſhall
Bewitch my ſoul to love :——O *Marciano*,
How I lament *thy fate :* heavens lend me tears,
Since by my prodigal expence of ſorrow,
I'me become banquerout : or elſe I beg
A period to my dayes : ſince certainly,
Life without love, is but calamity.　　　　　　　*Exit weeping.*

Scæna Septima. [*Scæna Quarta*]

Enter Manduco, Marionetta.

Mar. CAn he not ſpeak for himſelf, Sir ?　he muſt court by
　　　　his embaſſadours, forſooth.
Man. The reaſon is, *in promptu,* Madam ; for the youth is
endued with pudicity : he cannot be his own *buccinator*, or Trum-
　　　　　　　　　　　　　　　　　　　　　　　　　　　　　peter

petter of his own fame; but he bid me affure you that he did vehemently, *imo toto corde* affect you. And fo it may appear by his own manufcripts; as, *exempli gratia*, read the 3, *page*, 20th line of that luculent Epiftle of his to you, dated, 1. *Cal. Martii*; You will find that a man cannot expreffe himfelf more lovingly: he calls you, *enim*, the *prototype* of all beauty, the *Archetipe* of modefty, the fource from whence all other rivolets of chaftity do Scaturiat, *&c.* Is not that *amantiffimum* ?

Mar. No, 'tis not enough, Sir.

Man. No——why he told me, that you would not permit *ofculation*, and what elfe can he do when he is in privat with you, for I taught him not to be loquacious——

Chryf. Be merry, Sifter, you are happy, you } *Enter* Chryfoliare a Lady, Sifter—— } na *haftily.*

Man. A Lady !——*quid fibi vult*, to whom is fhe defponfat, Madam ?

Chryf. The bufineffe is now at a clofe, Sifter, *Caffio* may go to his travells now, he dare trouble you no more, Sifter.

Mar. What d'you mean ? fhall I be married, and not know to whom ?

Man. Yes, *Sicuti nunc mos eft*, you may be collocate } *Afide.* in nuptialls, before you know *cui, quando, & quomodo, id* } *eft*, to whom, how, or when.

Chryf. Don't you know, Sifter, *Signior Becabunga?*

Mar. Is he the man ? *Chryf.* Who elfe d'you think ?

Man. How now *omnia recte* again——Lady, I congratulat the immenfe, ineffable felicity and fecundity of your fagacious election——

Chryf. Hath not he been wooing you all this while ? who elfe fhould be your husband, but he, pray ? *Man.* Hum——

Mar. Well I am content. *Man. Recte*——

Chryf. Content,——marry I fhould willingly change conditions with you. *Man. Bene habet.*

Chryf. He is a good match, I'le affure you.

Man. I can add a jurament to that.

Chryf. Mr. *Manduco*, fhe owes much to you for it.

Man. To me, Madam : O I am obligate to your ingenuity.

Chry,.

Chryf. She does indeed, Sir:——Come, Sifter, let's in, and de-
vife what rare fancies wee muft have againft the wedding, wee'l
fend to the Mercers prefently, and have the best Sattins, taffatas,
ribbons and fuch other toyes, that can be had for money, come,
come, —— Farewell good Sir —— honeft *friend Manduco*,
farewell.

Mar. Well, he may be a good husband yet *for all that*——

Manduco folus   Exeunt.

Friend *Manduco*, faith fhe, *notatu dignum* : now am I their
friend, their amicall relation : fo, this matrimony is, I may fay,
now almoft, very nigh, altogether confummate : for which I
expect a large honorary from both parties : O the pregnant wit of
an intelligent Scholaftick ! now if I can effectuat the like for *Signior Pantaloni*, I fhall have likewife *aliquid amplius* : fo that I
muft at length provide for a matrimoniall relation to my felf : for,
although, I be *quinquagenarius*, or fifty years of age, yet what
Virgin in *Florence* will refpuat me when I abound in riches, and
fhall be——*Dives agris, dives, pofitis in foenore nummis.*

Exit.

Scæna Quinta.

Enter Pantaloni *with* Chryfolina.

Pant. NOw, Madam, fince I have got you all ⎫ *Embraces*
alone, I proteft, I muft make a little bold ⎰ *her.*
with you——*Chryf.* How, Sir !

Pant. In civility only, I mean in civility, Madam, for I would
only ask you one queftion, and that's not two, *videlicet*, whether or no, that is, when we may be *Joyn'd in the lawfull band
of matrimony, betwixt thefe parties following*, to wit. for you fee
Becabunga has not been long a doing, he has taken your Sifter to be
his lawfull fpoufe already, I hear, although he has been but a fort-
night a wooing of her, and yet I have been wooing *you* one time
with another thefe three moneths, I wot well, and I am fure that
you love me——*Chryf.* Are you fure, Sir ?

Pant.

Pant. Yes indeed, and I think there is as much reafon for the one as for the other : and to be free with you, a my confcience I might have had a bony Gentlewoman (juft fuch another as your felf) with twelve thoufand Duckats in portion, a moneth fince, had it not been for you : confider, pray you, what you promifed to my mother laft night.

Chryf. You will allow me a time to confult with my felf, Sir, will you not ?———

Pant. That's a ftrange confulting ! what have you been doing ever fince I fee you firft ? I am fure you have had time enough to confult all this while : and I'l tell you now, when your friends and mine have agreed, there's no time to confult, but prefently to be *matrimonyed*; you know that as well as I now.

Chryf. You will do well to prefs me no further at this time, Sir.

Pant. I'l let you alone for once then ; but, the next time I fhall come to fee you, you muft not confult any : for, to tell you truly, as I heard my mother fay, you may be glad of me for your huf-band——*Chryf.* Pray, no more, Sir.

Pant. And then, when I have fpent fo much money in wooing you, you will yet go, may be, and marry another. Fy for fhame.

Chryf. I fhall not marry while I give you an anfwer, Sir.

Pant. I, but as my mother fayes, it is good to be fure, if any other man fhould beat me out of my ftirrops now : I would come to a peel'd egg, would not I ? *Chryf.* no more of that, Sir.

Pant. I'l refer my felf to your own difcretion then——but, O !——I had almoft forgot, I vow, that's very well remembred ; was not I mounted on *Peg-a-fus* laft night ? (now this *Peg-a-fus* is the mufes horfe, he has wings and flyes, God blefs us) and what think you I have done ? marry you fhall hear what rare Verfes I have made. O ! Madam, are you there ? you are } *Enter* Mar. come in very good time ; I was juft a going to read } my Verfes, but you fhall hear an Anagram firft—— } *Takes out his* It is a pretty thing, Madam ; you can read and } *Verfes*, &c. write I warrand you ; fee you there your own name—— } *reads.* You fee,——

    Chryfolina (Anagram)
    You're even like a cherry.

I'l

I'l be judg'd if that be not pretty now : for, d'you fee, I have only borrowed fome four letters, or fo, out of, Madam, your Sifters
name, here, becaufe fhe is a nigh relation and may fpare them ; and
I have added two (I think) out of the *quicknefs of my felf.*

Chryf. Excellent indeed, Sir. *Mar.* Good, upon my word.

Pant. I, but you have not feen all yet ; here are brave Verfes
upon your name, *Madam Chryfolina.*

Chryf. An *acroftick.* Sir.

Pant. I, I, an *accurftick,* the fame. And thus it is——take
notice now.   }*reads.*

    Canft thou not fee, Pantaloni,   *there's the* C. *now.*
    How thy Miftris is fo bony ?

Now I am speaking to my felf as 't were.

    Revera, *fhe is even fuch,*
    You cannot match her, and that's much.

Now there is C. H. R. Y. that is *Chry.*

    She is handfom, neat and fine,
    O, now if fhe were but thine.

There's S. O. now that's *Chryfo :* now I am fpeaking to my felf
you muft underftand all this while.

    Live then in hopes, and know it is conftantly thy duty,
    Is alwayes, everlaftingly, to extoll and upbraid her beauty.

But, now take heed, here comes the tongue of the trump——

    Narciffus, Rofes, and every flower,
    All muft yield to her fair, rare, bright, fparkling colour.

That's *Chry-fo-li-na :* Now, is not that right now ? fay any of
you, if you dare, if thefe Verfes be not as good as any you have feen.

Chryf. Mar. They are extream good, Sir.

                      Enter Boy, rounds Pant. *in the ear.*

Pant. So, fo, tell him I come :————Ladies, I muft leave you,
but I will not go home yet : *Becabunga* hath fent for me to a
collation ; we'l drink both your healths e're we go to bed yet, and
to morrow I fhall fee *you* e're *you* can get on your petticoats, *Madam Chryfolina :* for, I muft be more familiar with *you,* fince I have
got fuch a good commodity of frequenting *you*——I fhall fhow
my mother all that has paft betwixt us, *Madam ;* So farewell.

                                Exit.

                                Mar.

Mar. How d'you like him, Sifter?

Chryf. As formerly. I find him a very difcreet Gentleman.

Mar. I would you had him for your husband.

Chryf. I fhould wifh that fame, *in a fair way*, Sifter.

Mar. Confidering efpecially, 'tis beft to marry while you are now in your prime.

Chryf. Right————for old maids are meer dogs-meat, they fpoil the trade of wooing————Go by————go by.   *Exeunt.*

Scæna Sexta.

Enter Marciano, Borafco.

Bor. 'Tis true, my Lord; yet, I don't much approve
Your Dukes fevere proceedings: *Florence* will not
Endure the lafh of Monarchy, like *France*
Or *Spain*: ————No, they muft be their own carvers.
————I hope the Lord *Barbaro,* who is now
Prefident of the Senate, will reform
Many of our abufes————*Marc.* Well, you will
Come all to tafte of your own vintage yet;
So I believe: for, never yet, rebellion
Efcap'd unpunifhed :————But, you remember
You promif'd that the Lady *Arabella*
Might fee me e're I dye. *Bor.* She fhall, my Lord;
————So————by this hand, a plot,   (*in going off.*
A very plot: he is my Rival fure————
But fhortly, *Signior*, you fhall carry your head
Upon a Scaffold; and then, who dares
Claim her, befides my felf.   *Exit* Bor.

Marciano *folus.*
When men begin to quarrel with their Prince,
No wonder if they crufh their fellow Subjects.
We are eye-fores to the State: their black defignes
Are crofs'd by us; and therefore we march off.————

          Enter Arabella *weeping.*
          G   *Marc.*

Marc. Am I not yet fufficiently plagued
With croffes : but you muft add one, which is
Heavieft of all,——why weeping——prethee ceafe
To vex thy felf : I am all refolution,
And long to fhow my courage : fince my ftars
Have ordain'd my departure : reft contented.
    Ar. Alas——and is my plot thus come to nought——
    Marc. Peace, prethee, for although I am not able
To pay what your perfections claim, yet fure
All generous fouls (*my true executors*)
Shall pay my debt, fair Nymph.   (*embraces her.*
    Ar. My Lord, your death can be no more couragioufly
Endur'd by you, then deplor'd by me——
    Marc. Tufh, as for death, I fear the varlet not,
I've often ftare'd him out of countenance :
I have confidered, that love to my Prince,
Should over-fway all others : have chofen
Rather t'endure one ftroke, and dye, then live,
And undergo the cenfure (of all crymes,
The moft deteftable) *Difloyalty.*
    Ar. Ay me ! incenf'd heavens, can nothing elfe,
Appeafe your wrath but fuch an offering ?
O, cannot I, (fpeak) I, although a woman,
Supply his place : I'le be an *Amazon,*
Expofe my naked breaft to fteel, and fhow
All women are not fetter'd to the diftaffe.
    Marc. Be not fo cruel : all good things forbid,
The world fhould fee fuch a fair foul expire,
And not diffolve it felf : thou cannot dye,
(Although thou wouldft) and *Marciano* live,
    No, no more then a watch can move, if once
The cord be broke : can I live after thee.
Ar. Alas, alas, unheard of tyranny !
Unjuft, even in injuftice : thus to be
So cruell, as to murder him, and yet
Spare me ; as much as if I fhould becom
My own foul murderer ; villains, how unjuft !

                                     But

——But here's my paffing bell. (*A bell rings within.*
I muft away——farewell——Oh, oh, my heart,
My heart diffolves, my Lord, I muft away.
  Marc. Away——farewell bright love—— (*embraces*
  Ar. Farewell, my Lord——
  Marc. Farewell——now all good things preferve thee here,
The gods hereafter : *thus*——and *thus* I leave (*kiffes,* &c.
My heart in legacy :——*thus,* I take my laft
Morfel of pleafure : never fhall my lips
Kifs any thing hereafter, fave the block——.
  Ar. So, *thus*——and *thus,* I willingly refign
All, what is yours, *this heart* : and fo farewell.
Farewell for ever——oh——Farewell, my Lord. *Exit.*
          Marciano *folus.*
——So, down goes duft and afhes, powers and honours,
Riches and joyes, the fmoak of our defires,
With all we can call ours : our youth, our ftrength,
Fly like the fullen clouds, when *Boreas* fwells
Their entrails with his breath : we fuddenly,
Like wilde-fire, difappear, and ftreight another
Steps in our place ; and fo we are no more——
—— Then heart, as thou haft ftill afford me courage,
  Infpire me now, that I may valiantly
  Act the laft part of this my Tragedy. *Exit.*

Actus Quartus, Scæna Prima.

Enter Manduco *folus, drunk.*

WHere is this fame unhappy Boy ? this *Signior Becabunga,*
I have been making inveftigation, fcrutination, explorati-
on, and fpeculation for him this hour, and yet I cannot find this *in-
dividuum vagum,* as I may fay——fo, what are (*Enter* Caff. Leon.
you, *boni viri,* I know, you have hurryed this Gentleman for whom
I fearch to fome compotation, or elfe *ad lupanar* ; yea, I am fure of

it——how fad it is to fee young men, even, *impuberes adolefcentes,* indulge venery, and ebriety fo much, & *quid Venus ebria curat?* as a friend of mine fayes.

Caff. The fellow's drunk, fure——

Man. ——Drunk ! O *pervicacem hominis indolem* ! accufing me of ebriety, when I am, even *in fana mente conftitutus,* conftitute in fanity of mind : 'tis true, indeed, I have been drinking; but it was with fome of my brethren, *imo fratres fratrerrimi.*

Leon. What were they ?

Man. Why, there was *Light-body, Laurie, Latie, Cheifly quoq ; Brounie, Bowiq ; Hi enim funt Tufcanii gloria fumma foli* : befides our *hofpes,* what d'you call him, *Architabernarius,* or Arch·taverner, who is one of the commiffioners for adminiftration of——*drink*——to the people of *Tufcania.*

Caff. Don't you enquire for *Signior Becabunga,* Sir.

Man. Yes, the very fame, where is he ? *ubinam eft ?*

Caff. You will find him at the *Verona tavern,* hard by, with fome of his comrades.

Man. Say you fo, I will go find him then, *profecto* I think I could fcarce abftaine from vapulating him for this his contumacy. *Exit.*

Caff. Now *Leonardo,* 'tis time we were ftirring, if we do not, this match will go on.

Leon. Nay, I'l do any thing for thee, e're thou lofe her, *Caffio,*

Caff. Come then ; I have almoft gull'd *Pantaloni* into a belief, that *Becabunga* wrongs him, for which he fwears he will be revenged : now, if you can do the fame with the other, our defign may fucceed yet.

Leon. Well, go you about your bufinefs then, fear not me.

Exit.

Caff. Now, wit and art affift us both, I'l fearch my gamefter and accomplifh the trick. *Exit.*

Scæna

Scæna Secunda.

Enter Arabella, *with the* Jaylor.

Jayl. MAdam, I will conduct you to him once again, but you muſt be very ſecret, for I hazard my life and reputation, if my Lord *Boraſco* have intelligence of this, for he gave me ſtrict command this morning, that I ſhould admit none to him but his confeſſor.

Ar. I ſhall be very ſecret, *I* warrand you.

Jayl. Come then, ſoft Madam, ſoft. } *Exeunt, ſhe enters*

Ar. For heavens ſake good my Lord, } *again with* Marciano
Vpon my knees I beg it———

Marc. This is impoſſible ; I cannot do it ;
Prove not a ſweet Remora any more,
I'me now reſolv'd : look to thy ſelf, fair gemme.

Ar. Cannot the tears of innocence prevaile.
Where is your courage now ? what ? are you cool ?
Is all that noble blood, that formerly
Run in your veines exhauſted ? muſt a woman
Become your Trumpeter, and ſtirr your ſpirits
Since 'tis but death at all hands———*Marc.* Prethee hold,
I would moſt willingly (as what man will doubt)
Procure my liberty by what ever meanes
But———O here lyes my fear, thou, thou bright love,
May come to ſuffer by it———*Ar.* Ah my Lord.
Conſider pray' that I have liberty
To go abroad at pleaſure : I have gain'd
The Lord *Boraſco's* favour : he will grant me
That which ſome dare not ask, nay muſt not think on.
I'le follow you without the leaſt ſuſpition.
Conſider that———*Strenuo* hath promiſed
To entertaine the *Jaylor* in his cups,
While you be ſafely eſcap'd. *Marc.* I'le hazard then :
Bright angel of my fancy, ſee you follow

Immediatly

Immediatly, for e're you fhould endure
'The rebells cenfure, I would rather forfait
A thoufand lives. *Ar.* Doubt not of that, my Lord.
Marc. Then once for all——O my good ftars direct me.
Ar. Farewell, my Lord, goodneffe protect you ftill } *Embraces*
Marc. Farewell pure quinteffence of my affection
Farewell, pray heavens grant us a joyfull meeting. } *Exit.*
Ar. Now, now at length, I hope he fhall efcape ;
O fupreme powers, affift him now, or never,
And eafe my foul of its long burning fever. *Exit.*

Scæna Tertia.

Enter Caffio, Pantaloni.

Caff. Sir, (as your friend I fpeak it) *Leonardo* and he have
joyn'd their wits together to affront you ; and you will
not beleeve what impreffion their falfe fuggeftions of you have
taken upon the Lady *Chryfolina.*

Pant. I! So I thought, when fhe told me laft day that fhe
would *confult* forfooth : A pox take all your confulting tricks,
fay I, for I never knew any good come of womens confultations
yet.

Caff. Right Sir, you might eafily fmell *Leonardo's* plot in that
fame word, for he intends that *Becabunga* fhall have *Marionetta*
and he himfelf *Chryfolina* : for which *Becabunga* does follicite
your Miftris all this while : if you look not to your felf quickly
you are undone, Sir.

Pant. I, fo I gueffed alwayes, for, d'you fee, fome women
are the moft humourous little creatures, a man fhall not know
when he is in their favour, and when not : but as for *Beca-*
bunga——I'le fay no more at this time : but I vow I'le cudgell
him to death fo foon as I can fee him.

Caff. And pleafe but command me, you fhall not want my affiftance, I'le affure you.

Pant. No Sir, I fhall not need your help to beat fuch a puppet
as

as he is: what would you think to write a challenge to him, Sir?

Cass. So you know, I advis'd you at first, when I sent for you to the *Taberna del Reina*, while you beleeved that *Becabunga* had sent for you.

Pant. Hang him, I will hear no more of him: I will write a challenge to him presently.

Cass. And if you'll please to take my advice in penning on't, I will so terrifie him.

Pant. With all my heart, Sir, for I would have it such language as might make him hang himself for fear: and for *Leonardo*, after I have discussed *Becabunga* then have at him.

Cass. If you please to employ me to carry it to him?

Pant. Yes Sir, you shall go along with me, and help me to write it, for the truth is I am not much us'd with such challenges, and my mother bid me allwayes have a care of quarrelling, but an she were burn'd I'le fight with that rascall, who has affronted me so.

Cass. A most generous resolution.   *Pant.* Come with me Sir.

Cass. Now, *Leonardo*, play thy game, or never   . ⎱*Aside.*
⎱
Exeunt.

Scæna Quarta.

Enter Marciano *solus, disguis'd as having escap'd.*

——THanks to my stars! as yet unknown
I have cheat all the sentinells; and now   ·
I suck free aire again:——you powers above
Direct my suddain course: and save my love.   Exit *quietly*
Within. Jayl. Ho, where's the pisse-pot there.

Str. Sirrah drawer, 'tother quart of sack, you raggamuffin you.

Courtain drawn appear Str. *and the* Jaylor,
drinking.

Jayl. You shall do me reason *Signior Strenuo:*——'tis my noble
Generals

Generals health, *Signior Strenuo*——Ho, where's the pifs-pot there?——you fhall drink it, *Signior*——

Str. Come then, we'll drink his good health, although he has but two dayes to live. *(drinks.*

Jayl. No matter for that, I love to be courteous to the laft breath, *Signior*; come, give me the cup: Sack, good *(drinks.* Sack, *Signior*——O brave Sack; come, let's have *(drinks again.* a catch, *Signior.*

Str. Come then——*Here's a health to the pretty little thing,*
With the bony, bony radiant eyes,
And the bony, bony, plump, round thighs ;
Let us fing——let us fing—— *(drinks.*

Jayl. Let us fing, let us fing——O brave *Strenuo*, here's a cup to thee for thy catch. *(drinks.*

Enter a Servant, *beckons to* Str. *Str. approaches to him.*

Ser. He is efcap'd. *Str.* 'Tis good, no more, filence I command you.

Ser. He waits for you. *Str.* Plague on you, no more I fay.

Ser. My Lord is efcap'd I fay.

Str. Pox take you, hold your peace, or you'l fpoil all I fay.

Jayl. Come young man, how does my noble General? you are his fervant, I know——here's to him, a brimmer of Sack. *(drinks.*

Str. Drink and be gone, you cocks-comb you——

Jayl. You fhall pledge me neighbour. *Ser.* I fhall, Sir. *(drinks.*

Str. My Lord has ordain'd me to prefent his love and refpects to all friends at my return to *Siena*——get you gone whorefon, get you gone, or you'l fpoil all. *Exit.* Ser.

Jayl. Well, he's a noble Gentleman, *Signior*, although I dare not fay it: but, no more of him, this cup is yours, *Signior*, we'll have t'other flaggon of Sack e're we part ; for I love to be merry as well as courteous, efpecially amongft ftrangers, *Signior*——Ho, drawer, Sirrah, Loggar-head, the pifs-pot, *(Courtain drawes* Baftard, fhall a man fpoil his breeches, you fon of a whore you.

Enter Strenuo *quietly with the* Servant.

Str. You puppet you, could not you hold your peace when I bid you——come, where is my Lord?

Ser.

Ser. At the *Colonna* in the *Strada del Popolo*, there he lurks quietly while you come to him.

Str. Let the rogue the Jaylor flip then, and we'll bid adieu to *Florence*; come, come quickly. *Exeunt.*

Scæna Quinta.

Enter Arabella *fola, traverfe quietly.*

——S O, now he's gone : O ! how my heart does leap,
My pulfe begins to move, fince now I know
He's paft the rebels reach, before this time.
All's well : this day, by order of the Senate,
Am I to be enlarg'd : had *Marciano*,
Whofe underftanding foul, div'd in the deepeft
Gulfs of fufpition, even but conjectur'd,
How e're they could accufe me for his flight.
Had rather died, e're he had condefcended
To any fuch attempt——but now he's fafe,
I'l follow clofe my felf : So hope affift me.   *Exit.*
    A noife within of many voices, crying confufedly.
        Souldiers fearching for Marciano.
        Enter Jaylor, *weeping and railing.*
Jayl. A pox on all your *Siennois* tricks, fay I, plague on that villain *Strenuo*: my noble General's gone, fled, gone : what fhall I do ? How the devil came I to be gull'd by that fame *Strenuo?* The laft night while he and I were deep in our cups, my noble General breaks the prifon and efcapes. O ! plague on his crazy cocks-comb, I could have trufted him affoon as any in *Florence*, and yet he hath played me fuch a trick as may bring⎫ *Within,* Jaylor, me to a ropes end yet——   ⎭ Jaylor, &c.
    Harke——my Lord *Borafco* fearching me, I fhall be hang'd without doom or fentence——
        Enter Borafco *with Souldiers.*
Bor. Where is this villain ? *Jayl.* Here am I my Lord.
Bor. You ugly fcarabe, what do you deferve ?
                            H   Sirrah

Sirrah, you ſhall be hang'd. *Jayl.* Alas! my Lord,
I was deceived, groſsly cheated, gull'd,
Fox'd and what not, by *Signior Strenuo* ;
A plague on him, may I ſay——*Bor.* Peace, you wretch,
My Lord *Barbaro* will cauſe puniſh you
For your negleſt, For he had ne're eſcap'd
Had he not bryb'd you——*Jayl.* I never ſee his coyn.
  Bor. Good gods! this day was he to be beheaded,
Now none knows where he is——this *Siennois* Lady
Will be examin'd : for ſhe ſeem'd to carry
A great reſpect to him : and (this I know)   (*aſide.*
The Senate will ſuſpeſt her acceſſory,
No doubt : ſo ſhe ſhall be condemn'd to die :
But I'l prevent their ſevere reſolutions
By all means poſſible——Come, you Scoundrel, come
You may be hang'd yet, Sirrah, e're all be done.
  Jayl. O! no more of that word *hanging*, my neck itches already.
                                    Exeunt.

Scæna Sexta.

Enter Leonardo, Becabunga.

Leon. C An you deſire any more? look you, Sir, a direſt challenge.
      Bec. I know not what belongs to your challenges ;
but I am ſure, as you ſay, he has affronted me.
  Leon. Sir, the very words of this challenge would encourage
one ; conſidering eſpecially, that he is the baſeſt coward that ever
breath'd for all this.   *Bec.* Think you ſo?
  Leon. Yes indeed, Sir, I warrand you he dare never appear in
field againſt you : he is but a bragging fellow.
  Bec. Nay, if I thought he would not appear, I might ſay ſomething.   *Leon.* Truſt me, Sir, he dares not.   •
  Bec. I, but d'you hear, Sir, if we can be handſomly reconciled,
what needs fighting?
  Leon. Fy, Sir, you cannot honourably refuſe, when he has writ
a challenge to you.   *Bec.*

Bes. Not, Sir, why cannot I write another to him, and call him a coward, a rafcal, a flave, a villain, and what not, and ftill preferve my honour, as you call it?

Leon. Alas! good Sir, there's no time now to talk, now you muft fight, and I will affift you.

Bec. I, if you will hold him to me while I beat him, there may be fomething on't too.

Leon. Doubt not, Sir; but, as I told you, he dares not appear, you have no more to do, but come arm'd to the fields, and if you find him not, brandifh your Rapier in the air thrice, proclaim him a coward, and fo return.   *Bec.* With my honour, Sir?

Leon. Yes, Sir, with your honour entire.

Bec. Well, I fee I muft fight; but if he doth not appear, now, I fhall be in a brave condition: for, then I will fwear, rant and domineer, by my word of honour, as my fathers foot-groom does. But will he not come, think you?   *afide.*

Leon. My life for't, he dares not appear; courage, we will out-dare both him and *Caffio.*

Bec. Well, but when all's done, Sir, betwixt you and me, were I at home in the Country again, all your honour, and honour above honour, fhould not caufe me fight: for, *Pantaloni* has learn'd to fence, Sir, and I know not what belongs to fencing, not I.

Leon. Tufh fear not him, I tell you, he dares not appear, and if he does, I'l fight him my felf.

Bec. Will you do fo, Sir, and I will be your *tres humble ferviteur Monfieur:* for d'you fee, Sir, I am to be married fhortly, now if I fhould chance to be kill'd, (as who knowes but I may) you know then, Sir, I cannot be marryed; why? becaufe I fhall be dead, that's a good reafon, Sir.

Leon. Plague on him for a coward, how he talks; I fhall have more ado to allure him to this duel, then a crack'd Courtier has to perfwade an Ufurer to become furety for him.   *afide.*

Bec. And then you know, Sir, *Pantaloni* is to marry the one Sifter, and I the other: now it is not fit that we fhould fight together, who are to be brethren fhortly, for I know not what.

Leon. Why, Sir, you muft refolve to fight: go along with me to the field : and if he offer to thruſt at you, I'le ſtep in betwixt, and ſave you both.

Bec. Will you be as good as your word, Sir ? *Leon.* I will indeed.

Bec. Then have at him——But harke you, Sir, you muſt have a ſpeciall care he touch not my face, for ſo he may put out my eye (God bleſſe us) and then where is your honour forſooth ?

Leon. He ſhall not touch you Sir, come, delay is dangerous.   *Exeunt.*

At the other end Enter Caff. Pant. *traverſe,* &c.

Pant. You may ſtand by, and ſee fair play, Sir, I ſhall beat him to ſome purpoſe : *Caſſ.* As you think fit, Sir.

Pant. Come on then——O *Becabunga* ! thou knowes not how nigh thy fatall hour approaches——for I am ſure he dares not appear.   *Exeunt.*

Scæna Septima.

Enter Arabella *ſola in Priſon, more cloſely confin'd then formerly upon the report that ſhe was to be beheaded.*

Ar. O gods ! is this the height of all your wrath :
     May I expeʄt a *requiem* in this ſtroak ?
Yes ſure——then graciouſly be pleaſ'd to hear
My ardent votes :——O may my blood appeaſe
Your incenſ'd mindes : reſtore my lawfull Prince :
Let *Marciano* live : Let nothing hurt him :
O hear him, hear him, if there be a faith
Able to reach your mercy, let him have it.
I plead none for my ſelf :——O love aſſiſt me,
Courage, beyond the ordinar of my ſex,
Support my ſpirits in this agony :
Death's but the thaw of all our vanity.   (weeps,

                                                        Enter

Enter Borafco *quietly.*

Bor. Nay now my foul diffolve : 'tis but a trouble
To keep thy quarter in this perplexed body.
O unkind Senate ! eyes have not feen a fairer
Modell of beauty——Sure, no hatchet dares
Be horfe-leech to her veines : or if it does,
All iron fhall be quite accurf'd hereafter.
—No, ther's an angell keeps that paradice
A fiery angell guards her : Vertue, vertue,
Ever, and endleffe vertue ! O rare beauty !
The neereft to her maker, and the pureft,
That ever dull flefh fhew'd us : fuch another
Could make attonement for half her fex.
——See how fhe weeps——   *Ar. Difcovers him.*
Ar ——So, now my torturer comes——
Bor. Now all good angells bleffe thee, faireft, trueft
Heart-ravifhing beauty : cruell, yet lovely tyrant.
Why ftill in forrow ? fhall I never have
One gracious fmile——Alas, how willingly
To fave thy precious life would I fubmitt
My neck to cruelty—by this hand, I would—— } *Kiffes her hand.*
Ar. Since it is ordained, Sir, I'le not endeavour
To prove a male-content. Sir, I have done
What I intended ; fhee's a cowardly Girle,
Who cann't endure one ftroke for him, whofe fafety
Is fo dear to his prince and country, vex not
Your felf for my misfortunes : nothing can
Affright my refolutions——
Bor. Strange love ! not to be parallel'd ?
Ar. Pifh—I contemn the fury of your bafe
Malicious fenate : reason does difdain
To dwell with fuch, whofe fouls are ftiffled with rage,
They fentence, whom they will, no matter why,
Since innocent, or guilty, we muft dye.
Bor. Madam, you fhall not dye I will follicit
The Senate for you : if I cannot prevaile
As I expeƈt, before it come to th' worft

I'ie

I'le fet you free, although their fury reach
My perfon for it——who does enterprife
To ferve his fancy, muft all feares defpife. } *In going off.*

 Ar. Ah vain fomenter of vain, fruitleffe hopes,   *Exit.*
Thy windmill-thoughts will break their axel-tree:
Go foolifh enterprifer: hope no favour
From one, who e're fhe fuffered thy embraces,
Would rather undergo a thoufand tortures.
——No, if e're woman was, or may be found,
That for fair fame, unfpotted memory,
For vertues fake, and only for it's fake
Dares challenge room in hiftory: O love
Let me be only Martyr in the cafe.
O *Marciano*, were it not thy fafety
That did fupport my foul, I fhould prevent
The executioner: but fince thou art
Free from the rav'nous clutches of the rebells,
Poor *Arabella* from that fpark alone
Derives her prefent courage——
——Then bleffed hour approach, I'le boldly fhow
That for his life, I can endure one blow.   (*Exit weeping.*

Scæna Octava.

Enter Caffio, Pantaloni, *Swords drawn.*

Caff. THis is the place, this is the hour appointed.
 Pant. Yes, Sir, but, you fee, he has not appear'd, may not
I put up my rapier now, and go home again with my honour, may
I not?
 Caff. Not Sir: you muft have a little patience.
 Pant. Ho, Ho, that's very true, I muft proclaime *Leonardo* and
him both cowards———*O yes*———*O yes*———
       One coughs, and whifpers within.
 But (a pox) I hear them comming hither. Come, *Signior*
Caffio, wee have tarried too long, we will now return.
               Caff.

Caff. No, no, ftay a little yet.

Pant. I fee this fellow has a mind I should be kill'd: would I had that unlucky challenge in my pocket again.

Caff. 'Slid, here they come; to your po- ⎫ *Enter* Leon. Bec.
fture, Sir.   ⎭ *fwords drawn.*

Bec. O! look you there's *Pantaloni*, Sir, and *Caffio* too, you faid he durft not appear.

Pant. Nay faith, now I fee 'tis no more jefting, there they come both with their Rapiers drawn. *Caff.* Courage, *Signior.*

Bec. What fhall I do now Sir? *Leon.* Fight, what else?

Caff. We'll fight all four at once. *Leon.* Yes, yes, by all means.

Caff. Have at thee then, villain *Leonardo.*   ⎫
Leon. At you, Sir.   ⎬ *Thruft.*
                                                    ⎭

Caff. Come, to't *Becabunga.*

Bec. Not I, Sir; as I am honest I will fight none at this time: for I have fome bufiness to do in the city, Sir.

Leon. What, you fneaking gull, will you not fight for your Miftris, Sirrah.

Bec. No, Sir, I will fight for no Miftris at this time; I muft go about bufiness of more importance, Sir——O! if he had *(afide.* not appear'd now. *Leon.* Not for the Lady *Marionetta*, Sir?

Bec. No, Sir, I will renounce all the right I have to her, before I fight, at this time at leaft.   *Pant.* I like that well.

Caff. 'Slid, fhall we come to the fields with you, and return thus affronted? fight it out bravely, or by this hand I'l run you both thorough.

Pant. Nay, it fhall not be fo, Sir, you fee we cannot fight at this time: for, the truth is, (now when I remember) I have an appointment too, within less than a minute of an hour hence, with fome Ladies of my acquaintance.

Leon. That's all one to us, Sir.

Pant. I fee I muft do it, there is no way elfe to efcape—— *(afide,* Gentlemen, I know what will please you: because we have brought you into the fields, that you may not be angry, as *Becabunga* fayes, I will renounce all the right I can have or claim in the Lady *Chryfolina.*   *Leon.* Good———

Pant. For, d'you fee, Sir, I care no more for her, then a Roarer does for his old Punk.   *Leon.* Excellent.   *Pant.*

Pant. I proteſt to you, Sir, I think they are fools that fight for women, let them fight for themſelves a Gods name, it is ſufficient we love them. *Leon.* Admirably good !

Bec. So I ſay too Sir, and if you have wrong'd me, I here freely forgive you.

Caſſ. Sir, that's not enough, you ſhall both ſeal this paper, that we may teſtifie to other Gentlemen, how we were ready to fight.

Bec. What paper, Sir ?

Leon. No matter for that, Sir, you ſhall both ſeal it, or by theſe hilts———

Pant. Nay hold, good Sir, I ſhall ſeal it,———what terrible oaths theſe fellowes uſe.   (Pant. *ſeals.*

Caſſ. Come, you muſt ſeal too. *Bec.* Yes, yes, Sir.   (Bec. *ſeals.*

Leon. Now get you gone both of you for a brace of infamous puppets, cowardly cocks-combs, you arrogant, empty-skull'd wittals, not worthy of the leaſt favourable ſmile from any Lady: you have reſign'd your intereſts in two honourable Ladies, and therefore deſerve no leſs then to be kick'd———thus to be kick'd———   (*kicks him.*

Pant. What d'you mean, Sir ?

Caſſ. Thus to kick you, you brace of baſtardly Baboons———

Leon. And ſo we leave you as we found you, a pair of impudent filchers of reputation, not worthy name of Gentlemen.

Caſſ. Farewell my Cob-webs———

Leon. Farewell good Spanniels, farewell———   *Exeunt ambo.*

Pant. Marry pox take you both, what notorious raſcals are they.

Bec. Come, come, we muſt be friends again; let them go hang themſelves if they pleaſe.

Pant. If I had them in another place———

Bec. But harke you, what if they ſhow the Ladies that we have renounc'd our intereſt in them ? what ˙ will you ſay then ? think you that ever the Lady *Chryſolina* will look upon you again.

Pant. I ſhould have made them both black and blew.

Bec. Will you let's go and prevent them, I ſay.

Pant. By all means———this trick ſhall do *Leonardo* no good, what a fool was I to believe *Caſſio.*

Bec. So I ſay alwayes ; but come, quick———he that ſpeaks firſt is alwayes beſt heard.

Pant.

Pant. I'l to them yet, for all this, he has not beat me out as he thinks. *Exeunt.*

Scæna Nona.

Enter Marciano *folus, having got intelligence that*
Arabella *was to die.*

——HEart! art thou thunder-proof? can nothing break thee?
  Shall *Arabella* die, and thou ftill live?
——Burft ftubborn peece of flefh——O! heavens forbid,
Thofe eyes may live to fee the world without her.
——The Senate hath condemn'd her——O! bafe wretch!
Unhumane Tyrants; Monfters of this age;
O! barbarous villany; what bloody thoughts?
It is not becaufe fhe was acceffory
To my efcape: No fure, but 'caufe I love her,
That fhe muft die; as if thofe hell-hounds mean'd
To ftrike the Stars, and all good things above,
Regardlefs of her deity; no devil
Could be more cruel——But, hold, *Marciano,*
Thou ar't the executioner: thou alone.
Say, wretched man, was thou affraid to die?
Could fear prevail fo far? Alas! thy fame
Has loft it's right wing by thy too rafh flight,
Leaving fo rare an hoftage in thy place.
Yet, who had faid, or who had ever thought,
A thing fo clofely carryed could have ever
Thus come to light. She was to be enlarg'd
That very day: for fo fhe did affure me,
Elfe had my wearied foul refign'd it's casket,
And I, by this time, fteep'd with bleffed fhades
Of my Anceftors, maugre all her tears.
——But what, I dream, I muft do fomething more
Then only mourn for her: if art affift,

I   I I

I'l ſtudy to preſerve her ; either return,
Submit my ſelf to mercy of the Rebels,
If otherwayes thoſe goblins cann't be conjur'd,
Or elſe by open force, or private means.
What e're be th'event, I'l procure her freedom :
May be the gods are more propitious
Then I imagine.   Come——it is reſolv'd
She ſhall not die——fools are amaz'd at fate,   } *in going off*
Griefs but conceal'd are never deſperate.

Exit.

Aƈtus Quintus, Scæna Prima.

Enter Boraſco *ſolus.*

N Ay hold, my ſpleen ; do not burſt yet——
　 How this ſame Lady hath abus'd my favour,
Eſcap'd, no man knows how ; gone, God knows whether.
If I fly not, I ſhall ſupply her place,
That is reſolv'd I know——Fortune, you ſhall not
Play upon me ; although you now begin
To frown upon moſt of our Senators :
For, ſince the brave Lord *Barbaro* is dead,
All ſuch as were his creatures are diſcarded ;
Amongſt whom, I am one—— a plague on all
Your baſe ſeditious cocks-combs : your proceedings
Will ſtrengthen *Cleons* intereſt.   Hell-hounds, Tygars,
Adieu baſe Elves : I'l poſt to *Venice* ſtraight,
And there evite the ruine of your State.

Exit.

Scæna

Scæna Secunda.

Enter Pantaloni, Becabunga, *with* Chryfolina, Marionetta.

Pan. Tu⌐h, these are all but ⌐tories, Madam, I was but je⌐ting with them when I did it.

Mar. Sir, I will hear no excu⌐e. *Bec.* I vow 'tis true, Madam.

Pant. Nay, but harke you, Madam *Chryſolina*, if you come to that with it, I can make you love me yet, whether you will or no.

Mar. Will you, Sir? *Chryſ.* Pray, how do you that, Sir?

Pant. Why, thus I in⌐truɛt it, Madam; I can ⌐how you ⌐e- veral Letters under your own hand and ⌐eal, day and date, *&c.* that you are my humble ⌐ervant, which you dare not for your ears deny, dare you? *Chryſ.* You had be⌐t be ⌐ilent.

Pant. Nay more, I know you love me yet, becau⌐e the la⌐t time I was with you, you gave me a knot of Ribbons, which my mother keeps well lock'd up in her Cabinet yet, as a love-token: and more- over, when I ⌐aid I will come and ⌐ee you again to morrow, you ⌐aid, ⌐ayes you, you ⌐hall be welcom.

Chryſ. This will not do it, Sir, you have renounced us, and therefore——— (*ſhe offers to remove.*

Bec. Nay hold, Madam, we were but in je⌐t.

Pant. And then they forced us to do it.

Bec. I, and if we had done it, they ⌐wore (God ble⌐⌐e us) that they would kill us.

Pant. And then, you know, it was better to ⌐eal a peece of paper then to be kill'd.

Chryſ. What ⌐trong arguments they u⌐e.

Mar. Si⌐ter, we must ⌐hake e'm off now or never.

Bec. And then, Madam, if we had been kill'd———

Pant. Yes, if we had been kill'd, it had been ⌐mall advantage for you.

Bec. I, and then, Madam——and then, I ⌐ay, Oh! if } *aſide.* *Manduco* were here to plead for me now.

Pant. Nay, if you will not hear us, take your pleafure.

Chryf. No more, Sir, get you gone, henceforth I difclaim you.

Pant. And I you too, d'you fee; I care no more for you, Miftris, then you do for me : I am as good a Gentleman as your felf; and if you were not a woman I would tell you more of my mind.

Bec. I knew it would alwayes come to this at length, I vow; I think you Gentle-women do nothing but entertain us with vain hopes for a while, and then caft us off.

Pant. Miftris, fhall I tell you, there are more Ladies in *Florence* then you that will be blyth of me yet; and fo long as I have money in ftore, I am fure to have Miftreffes in ftore.

Chryf. Are you fo, Sir ?

Pant. I that I am : but I will complain to your Uncle, to the Lady *Saromanca,* and to all your kindred, that you have cheat me, for all your fair promifes.

Chryf. You are a prating fool.

Pant. I am no more prating then your felf, Miftris ; but |if there be juftice to be had of you, I'l have it.

Mar. Come, let us leave them, Sifter, elfe they'll both fall a weeping.

Pant. For whom, for you, Miftris ? I'l let you know we are no fuch children.

Bec. No, but, I proteft, I cannot but weep though.

Chryf. Mar. Farewell, farewell, march to your travels my Gamefters, farewell.   *Exeunt ambo.*

Pant. Peugh——Farewell ; I believe you. are the greateft fool of the two, *Madam Chryfolina,* call they you.

Bec. I proteft, *Pantaloni,* I am very forry for the lofs of this bony Lady though. O ! how my father will chide me now : for he had given *Manduco* orders to provide my Wedding-cloaths, and now all's blown up.

Pant. Come, come, we know the worft on't : let them go, we will never want great matches yet ; let us think now to be revenged on them villains, *Caffio* and *Leonardo* : the firft time I meet any of them, I will cut the tongue out of their heads that they fhall never talk more.

Bec.

Bec. I, fo will I too : but we muſt have *Manduco* with us then, for he will make them ſtand in awe of him.

Exeunt.

Scæna Tertia.

Enter Marciano, *folus, as at* Piſa.

THat ſhe's eſcap'd, that, I know certainly,
    So letters from *Siena* have inform'd me.
But by what means, or where ſhe is, I know not.
Never remembers him, who, if he ſhould
Forget her but one hour, would think he had
Offended highly, yet ſhe's ſilent ſtill.
If I receive no letters from her, ſhortly,
I'le become jealous of her, ſure ; that ſhe,
Who was all love, is now ſo quickly cold
In her affections.————But what ! I blaſpheme
The vertuous *Arabella*, ſhe's all vertue,
And cannot prove unconſtant ————
Now let me meditate on what my Prince
Hath order'd me to do : He's ſtill the ſame,
And bears a mind that floats above the waves
Of all adverſities, as who ſhould ſay,
Fortune, even do thy worſt. His Counſellours,
Like to wiſe Marriners, affray'd to ſtretch
The top-ſayles of their courage in this tempeſt,
Leaſt both they, and their Prince ſhould ſuffer ſhipwrack.
Only was I commanded ſome years ſince
Upon an expedition to *Siena*,
Encourag'd by th' affectionate expreſſions,
And actions of the valiant *Caſſanæo*,
And others of our loyal country-men.
But fortune cruſh'd our enterpriſes, ſo
I did return to *Savoy*, where my Prince
Did then reſide : and now, I am commanded

To

To fecond here an enterprife at *Pifa*,
Which whether it fucceed or not; my duty
Is yet at leaft to profecute it——   *A poft-horn founds within.*
How's this——a poft-horn : good——

Enter Strenuo *with a Letter.*

Str. All's well, my Lord, now do our joyes begin.
To flourifh after fuch a tedious winter.
The Duk's reftor'd, and now intends at *Florence*.
Here, here's a letter for it, from himfelf.

    Marc. Reftor'd !—Nay hold my heart—I'l read this letter.   (*reads.*
——True, True :——O fortune how I hugge thee now.
And thou my good friend *Strenuo*——   (*embraces him.*

    Str. Brave dayes, my Lord; the Court does fill apace,
The Ladies croud in throngs : the glory of
Her fex, your darling, the fair *Arabella*,
Since clouds of melancholly are overblown,
Does now appear in loves full horizon.

    Marc. O how propitious ! lend me moderation,
Reins to my joy, as well as to my forrow,
Elfe, I fhall quickly burft to death : this bleff'd,
And unexpeéted *Tarantula* : of news
So ticles all my fenfes :——joyfull tidings !
My Prince reftor'd ! my deareft *Arabella*
At Court ! now my felicity lacks nothing
But fight to be compleat : that my eyes may
Perfwade my yet almoft incredulous foul,
To what my fancy never durft have prompted
——To horfe——To horfe, I'le poft to *Florence* quickly.

Exit. poft-horn founds.

Scæna

Scæna Quarta.

Enter Pantaloni, Becabunga, *and* Manduco
with swords by their sides.

Man. O *Tempora*! *O mores*! O the effrænate, licentious perverfity of untamed adolefcency! what a villanous, fcelerate attempt to entice two young Gentlemen to a Duel: who befides, that they are both innocent Boyes, why, their very Uncles and other friends, are employed in ferious negotiations of the Senate. *Proh Deum, atque hominum fidem*! Is all my induftry in follicitation, my immenfe ftudy and lucubrations for framing familiar epiftles, my oratory in private commendations and exhortations for both thefe Gentlemen come to nought!— *Proh facinus ingens*!

Pant. Peace, Mr *Manduco*: you muft not only teach us how to beat, but likewife affift us in beating thefe diffolute fellows ; for I have fworn, Sir, and that is enough——

Bec. I, fo I fay too, for, you know we wear our fwords here for no other end ; look you, are not my hilts very handsome, O now, I will fwear, *By thefe hilts*, as well as *Leonardo* himself.

Man. And for that effect, I have got my fword too : I am *lenis in puniendo* : but when I am provoked, *invenient me leonem*, they fhall find me a very Lyon : my fchollars at *Sancto Burgo*, where I was sometimes *ludimagifter*, can yet teftifie that : and for my feverity *in caftigando*——*Probatum eft.*

Pant. Although *Leonardo* has got my Miftris, yet I'le have about with him, albeit he be a Senatours fon in law, with a mifchief to his heart, when fuch Gentlemen of eftates as I, am fhak'd off.

Bec. And for me, fince *Caffio* has got my Miftris: let him keep her ; I muft look out for fome other great match in time ; for they fay, *Manduco*, that now fince the Duk's reftor'd, they who were active in the late rebellion, must be forfeit of their eftates : and
what

what will become of my Patrimony then : for you know my father has been a great man all this while, (I fear he never be so
again) now, you know, if I lofs my Eftate, how fhall I have a wife
then ? what think you, *Pantaloni* ? (Pant. *draws.*

Pant. Nay, I can think on nothing now, but how to thruft at
Leonardo.

Bec. So, I will draw too, if you come to that with it. (Bec. *draws.*

Man. And for me——I love no dimi-⎤ Man. *puts the hilts of*
cation——but when I am provoked, I ⎟ *his fword betwixt his*
will affift you——*Et fic arma amens ca-* ⎬ *feet, and tuggs at it vi-*
pio, nec fat rationis in armis, ⎦ *olently.*

Enter Caffio, Leonardo, *with* Chryf. Mar.

Caff. Madam, my refolution was alwayes unfeigned⎤
to ferve you : your coy refufal diminifhed nothing of ⎟ *to Mar.*
my affeftion, but did rather incite me the more to love ⎬
you. ⎦

Mar. I did alwayes efteem my felf honoured⎤ Bec. *runs away,*
in your love, Sir, though the capricious humors ⎟ Man. *and* Pant.
of my felf-feeking friends did countermand my ⎬ *retire to a corner*
defires. ⎦ *of the Theatre.*

Leon. Nay then, unfpotted beauty, anfwer thofe⎤
gracious obligations your felf : it passes the activity of ⎟
my invention. I have been alwayes your devout ad- ⎬ *to* Chryf.
mirer; but now I am fo much bound to love you, that ⎟
although my affeftion fhould fuper-erogat, yet I can ⎟
plead no merits. ⎦

Chryf. Sir, your merits have made conquest of my affections——

Caff. Prethee, *Leonardo,* would'ft fee⎤ Pantaloni *and* Man.
good fport—— ⎟ *juftles,* Pant. *wreftles*
Leon. As how ? ⎬ *loofe,* Man. *folus to*
Man. Nay, you muft ftay, I will not⎦ Caff. *and* Leon.
fight alone.

Pant. Fy, not before women, Sir, that were unhandfom——
Exit. Pant. *running.*

Man. Keep off, *boni viri*; for, if you approach, you fhall find
the vinegar of my wrath. I have chaftifed many fuch in my time,
I'l make you know what it is *rem habere cum Profeffore,* to bell
the cat with one to whom you owe refpeft. *Leon.*

Leon. *takes hold on* Man.

Leon. Thou flovenly, greazy Pedant, glafs-gazing, fuperfinical affected peece of ignorance, get you gone, fpeak no more ill of Gentlemen; or if you do, you may come to carry your joynts in a box yet——*Man.* Never again, Sir—— *(lets fall his fword.*

Leon. If you do——*Man. Ita me Deus amet,* never, Sir.

Caff. We'll put you to the ftripado, if you don't behave your felf more civily.

Man. Never again, as I am erudite—So help me, God——nevet.

Exit.

Mar. Poor fellow, he muft have his humour.

Chryf. If he could hold his peace fometimes, he is a good honeft fellow; but he can fpeak good of no man, but thofe of his own profefsion.

Caff. We have punifhed him fufficiently, let's think no more upon him.

Leon. Nor upon our *quondam* Rivals either. Come, we'll continue our progrefs to Court.

Exeunt omnes.

Scæna Quinta.

A joyfull noife within, Trumpets, Ketle-Drums, Ho-boyes, with all fort of mufick.

Enter the Duke, Marciano, *with others of the Nobility,* Courtiers *and* Attendants, *at his entry.*

Song.

Now breaks our day,
  Fairies away,
  Pack hence, I fay,
    Your power's undone.
Room for Jov's progeny,
Full of Divinity.

K

Cleon,

Cleon, *brave* Cleon, *natures Paragon,*
   Rebellion breathlefs lyes,
   Hell fings her obfequyes,
      Vfurping Traytors quick be gone.
Now, Cleon, *divine* Cleon *mounts His Throne,*
Rooin—room—room—room for Him alone.

Cleon. Heavens yet are juft : they now have paid us home
Our former loffes with large intereft———
——— A good while loft is never known to many,
An ill while feel'd is fcarcely known to any :
For men, like butter-flyes, rufh on the candle
Of war at all occafions, untill fome
Are burn'd to afhes : others hurt their wings ;
Then they recoil amaz'd, and not while then,
They blame the projects of their troubled brain.
——Now (gods affume our thanks) we, who before,
Were tofs'd in waves of war, are fo no more———
——*Florence,* take heed, jeft not with fupreme Powers,
'Tis hard to thrive, when heavens do countermand
Thy foul defigns :——But wifely learn to know
Thy former errors, and commit no moe.
   1. *Court.*——A Prince's word is good divinity——
   2. *Court.*——While Subjects oaths are down-right perjury,
And ferve for nothing but to feed Rebellion.
   Cleon. How ! *Marciano,* you feem difcontent,
What fullen cloud amid'ft this calm of joyes
O'rcafts your noble foul ?——*Marc.* Not I, dear Prince,
I am not difcontent.
   Cleon. Come, *Marciano,* you fhall feaft your fenfes
On what we know your foul entirely loves.
——Now let us in, 'tis time we were at counfell.

                       Exeunt omnes.

        Within, mufick as before.

           Song.

Dull man, do'ft not fee in his countenance
   Such rare becoming grace,

                          As

As one might freely say he did enhaunce,
Majesty in his face.
Why art become
So grossly dumb ?
Cannot thy tongue pay tribute to his praise ?
Harke how all Florence sing,
In such a cheerfull spring,
And every one their voices raise.
Why silent then, when after all our tears,
Clouds which did shroud the light, our Sun appears ?
Appears————Appears
Dissolving all our jealousies and fears.

Scæna Sexta.

Enter Arabella *sola.*

Ar. ALl now rejoyce, but I : my former griefs
Still dwell with me, untill the noble, constant,
Generous *Marciano* doth appear————
——Goodnefs ! 'tis he——O ! ⎱ *Enter* Marciano *discoursing quiet-*
how my heart begins, ⎰ *ly with a* Courtier.   Exit. *Court.*
Even as a murder'd carcaffe, to diftill
Grofs drams of blood at fight o'th murderer.   (Marc. *difcovers her.*
Marc.——Cold vertue guard me——if I dream not ——'tis fhe.
——Mercifull heavens, can *Marciano* fee
His very foul ? yet not in extafie.
——O ! *Arabella*, faireft, ever worthy,   (*embraces her.*
I offer thus my heart——thus——thus——and thus————
O ! art afsift me——fuddain joy had never
Suddain exprefsion——*Ar.* Sure, my Lord, you cannot
Be more furprifed then I am ; pray imagine
A heart abftract from cares, and hois'd in high
Raptures of joy ; even fuch you may define,
Mine-thine——thine-mine——the gods could ne'r have been
K 2   More

More gracious then now——
Then, *thus*, my Lord, pray let me evidence
The temper of my heart, fince you went hence. } *embraces*

Marc. O! thou, the loadftone of my elfe-wandring fancy,
That keeps my foul ftill fix'd——What can I render
Conform to thy fair merits——*Ar.* Love, my Lord,
——Love, love——I fay, I cannot ask for more.
Next, if you will oblige me, prethee honour
Our Friend *Falaffo*, one deferves your favour.
——He entertain'd me kindly in your abfence,
During your long exile. *Marc.* Heavens thank him for it,
I fhall efteem him highly, and recommend
Him to the Duke——But now, my heart's in flames——
——Never was man more happy in his choyce
Then I in mine——*Such Miftriffes are rare*—— } *afide.*
You were my fellow fufferer ; fprightly Nymph,
If love connive, would you not willingly
Be fharer with me in my profperity ?
Ar. Thofe, who know all things, know my great ambition.
Marc. No more——no more——we wrong our joyes to ftay
On fuch difcourfe——'tis time we fupplicate
The gentle *Hymen*, he fhall us unite,
That *Florence* may behold our joyes compleat.

Exeunt.

Scæna Vltima.

Enter two of the guard with Partuyfans.

1. *Part.* COme, Come, all things will now refume their ancient fplendour.

2. *Part.* Yes, yes, now we begin, like Marriners after a tempeft,
to fuck our bottles at eafe again.

1. *Part.* O brave dayes ! who would have dream'd on this
fuddain revolution fome years fince.

2. *Part.*

2. *Part.* No more of that difcourse, look to the Court-gates, for there fhall be such a crowd of Gallants with their Ladies, Apprentifes with their Wenches, Citizens with their Wives, and all the confufed rabble, by and by, that we fhall have a great labour on't to keep the half on'em out.

1. *Part.* Right, for the Lord *Marciano* is to be marryed to night, and we fhall have a Mafque, I warrand you.

2. *Part.* I beleeve we fhall have a merry night on't.

1. *Part.* You ar welcome, my mafters, walk ⎱ *Enter* Caff. Leon. towards the further corner, pray you, there ⎰ Chryf. Mar. you fhall have best room.

Caff. The Duke will be here by and by.   1. *Part.* We expeft fo, Sir.

Leon. Come then, wee'l afide, *Caffio.*

A flourifh within, Mufick, &c.
Enter moe Partuyfans.

Part. Clear the way, the Dukes a coming.

Enter Cleon, *leading* Arabella *by the hand,*
Courtiers, Attendants, &c.

Cleon.——— Remember no more, fair Lady,
On by gone miferies———   ⎱ Caff. Leon. Chryf. Mar.
                                          ⎰ *kifs the Dukes hand, &c.*

Enter Marciano *with* Strenuo, *prefents him to*
the Duke, &c.

Marc. May it pleafe your Highnefs ———
This was my friend, my very trufty friend
In all my exigencies, very kind
To both me and the Lady *Arabella.*
Here only, I prefent him to your Highnefs———   (Str. *kneels,* &c.

Cleon, Whatever favours were beftow'd on you,
We do account them done to our felves———
——— You are his friend, fo, *Signior,* you are ours.   (Str. *arifes.*

Str. May all the bleffings of the heavens combine
To raife your highnefs to a pitch divine———

Cleon. My Lord *Marciano,* we have alwayes had
A narrow eye over all your proceedings,

We've

Wee've found you loyall, without fpot or blemifh,
Valiant, at all adventures, ever faithfull,
And therefore after mature deliberation,
We here entruft the Government of *Siena*,
Your native country to your managing——
Here's our Commiffion——take it, and remember   } *gives him*
Our *honour* and the *humours* of *Siena*.   } *a Patent.*
    Marc. Great Prince, whofe daring eye ftrikes traytors dumb,
Revives all loyal fouls : difperfes all
Rebellions foggy mifts : you have this day
Conferr'd fuch honour on your highnefs fervant,
As were I a bafe Infidel, yow'd perfwade
My heart to faith, my tongue to oratory——
——Thus——thus, dear Prince, I tender folemnly,
All homage to your highnefs, while I dye.
    Cleon. Arife, enjoy thofe honours, and approve   } *Cleon takes him*
Your felf a pattern of both fear and love.   } *by the hand.*
    Man.——*Sereniffime, Auguftiffime——dux* } *Enter* Man. Bec. Pant.
    Court.——Remove, remove that fellow.   } *Strenuo prefents them*
    Part.——Come——come Sirrah, you think } *feverally to kiffe the*
you are in your fchool. *Man. Dux.*—— } *Dukes hand.* Man.
                                    harangues.
    Part. Come you villain.   } *Part. dragges*
    Man. Princeps——*Tus*——*Tus*——*caniæ.* } *him off.*
    Court. What an impudent rogue is this ?
    Cleon. ——As for this Lady, whom thy gentler fates
Have ftill referved for your chaft embraces,
We ftill will honour her, as having feen
Evident figns of her affection,
And loyalty to us——
    Ar. And ftill fhall be,
Dear Prince, fo much as in a Woman lyes,
I'le offer prayers and tears, and facrifice,
The firft fruits of my wifhes ; I'le implore
Such bleffings, as the gods have heap'd in ftore,
May rain upon your royal highnefs head,
That in your eyes heavens favours may be read——

                                          1. *Court.*

1. *Court.* May forrein Princes his great power envy———
2. *Court.* May he his treacherous enemies plots defye———
Leon. May he reftore our former happinefs———
Caff. And *Medicis* great princely houfe encreafe———
Marc. While all his faithfull Subjects long to fee
The royal hopes of his pofterity———
   All.———*Long live our Prince, and may he ftill appear*
       The brighteft Star in all our Hemifphære.
         A joyfull noife within, &c.

                        Exeunt omnes.
                        Plaudite.

F I N I S.